OUTLAWS IN THE SADDLE!

The moment Will Roman jailed the rustler, Jack Carstairs, the Box F ramrod knew he'd have trouble with Sam Engstrand's rival ranch crew. Engstrand was lynch-minded, but Roman wanted no necktie law in the new Montana range.

Even as he and his Box F crew were blocking the Engstrand men, another group of rawhiders broke Carstairs out. That changed the whole picture for Will Roman. It meant that Carstairs was no lone wolf, that the rustlers were organized—and that Will Roman was in for a shooting war with no holds barred.

A WESTERN NOVEL

SUNDOWN BASIN

RAY TOWNSEND

Author of "Gold Town Gunman"
and "Stranger From Texas"

WILDSIDE PRESS

CHAPTER I

Rain had fallen steadily for three long days and nights, but the drenched and running land, as though gasping for breath, lay resting in this evening hour. Above, great masses of cloud, like surly bruised giants, roiled fitfully, allowing but occasional passage to the feeble light of a sickly moon. Slowly, out of this vast, wet darkness, and into the yellow edges of the town's first light, rode a steadily jogging cavalcade of five weary men.

Will Roman, foreman of Ben Fowler's Montana Boxed F holdings, slouched in the saddle at the head of the group as it entered the street. Looking neither to the right nor the left as men stopped to stare from the walks, he led the procession past the Judith City Hotel, Newton's Mercantile and Sid Patterson's Lone Star Saloon. No one on the street spoke out. The only sounds that came were the creaking of saddles, the tiny metallic jingle of a loose spur, and the steady, sucking cadence of hoofs in the street's deep mud.

As the line of riders passed Patterson's, a single man stepped out through the swinging doors. For the space of a breath he surveyed the moving file. Turning quickly then, he raised his voice as he moved back into the saloon.

"It's Carstairs, by thunder!" They've brought in Jack Carstairs, tied to the saddle!"

Roman gave no sign that he had heard the cry, or noticed the rush from saloon to street. Twin furrows deepened between his brows when, farther on, he drew up at the rack before the squat frame building that housed the sheriff's office and jail. It was a new building, as were most in the town. It was a new country, in fact, and as Roman stepped down heavily from the saddle he felt disgusted because so recently settled a territory already found need for a building with cross-barred windows and doors.

Though barely turned thirty, Will Roman now bore the appearance and manner of a much older man. The past three days in the saddle had rounded the slope of his shoulders and slowed movements habitually more brisk. The dejection he had borne throughout the ride into town deepened as he glanced at the others. The sight of Jack Carstairs, slumped forward over hands that were bound to the horn of his saddle, brought a fleeting grimace of distaste to features weathered an ageless hue beneath his dark stubble of beard. He was a big man, Roman, tall and broad of chest, though he bore his weight slackly as he nodded at the man beside Carstairs.

"All right, Dusty. Let's get him inside. No sense in putting on a show for the town."

Dusty Wilson, small, wiry, towheaded and tophand under Roman on the Montana Box, leaned from the saddle, knifeblade glinting in the light from Newton's store. With a quick, flickering movement he freed the bound man's hands, which fell limply away. Without this support, Carstairs lurched forward and would have fallen had not Wilson reached out to clutch his shoulder. At this, Carstairs glanced up, looking about with dull, disinterested eyes. He was a darkly handsome young man with an air of furtiveness about him. Replacing his hands upon the pommel, he tilted his hatted head forward once more. Both of the two remaining riders owned small ranches in the Judith Basin, and one, Henry Freeman, nodded at the jail's dark front and spoke down to Roman.

"Looks like the sheriff ain't in, Will. Reckon we better wait till he comes?"

The elderly rancher's thin, habitual note of complaint grated against Roman's nerves. He was reaching up to pull Carstairs from the saddle when a deep voice stopped him.

"What's this, Roman? How come you to bring this coyote into town?" Sam Engstrand, owner of the Rocking Chair brand, planted himself at the edge of the walk in front of the jail. He was a bull of a man, about fifty, but in the full prime of his physical life. A small crowd of onlookers, coming up from store and saloon, gathered behind the huge rancher. Engstrand said, louder, "What the hell's the idea, Roman? You ain't got no wild notion of sending this ranny down to Miles City for trial?"

Roman let his gaze linger upon the big rancher for the briefest of moments, then turned again to Carstairs. "Come on, Jack. You'll be better off inside. I'll have one of the boys send over to the hotel for a meal."

He lifted his hand to grip the man's arm. Carstairs jerked free. His head came upright and he surveyed the bunch on the walk, suddenly defiant.

"You know damned well I wouldn't last out the night in that crackerbox jail!"

"You'll last all right, Jack." The pointed accusation and injured innocence in Carstairs' words added to Roman's irritation. He gripped the man's belt and pulled him from the saddle. He pushed him toward the walk as Wilson swung down behind. He said, "Dusty, see if you can pry Brady loose from Sid's bar long enough to open up one of his cells."

As the wiry little tophand went off in search of the sheriff, Roman nudged Carstairs up across the walk to the jail. Though no light showed within, the door of the sheriff's office gave beneath his hand. He pushed Carstairs in, striking a light as he entered. He touched the match's flame to the wick of the lamp on the desk and turned. Engstrand and several others had come through the door behind him.

"All right, gents," he said, noting that Carstairs had taken a stand against the barred door of the corridor that led to the cells further back. "Show's over. You can attend to your regular business now."

Several of the men glanced at Engstrand, as though expecting some qualification of Roman's dismissal to come from him. Nor were they disappointed. The huge rancher's heavy features were red with anger at having been so summarily ignored. He jutted his chin at Will.

"Not by a damn sight it ain't over, Roman. We're in

this thing togther, the whole danged bunch of us. Me
and my boys been combing the hills these last three
days as much as you, and I'll have my say. The whole'
thing was my idea in the first place. And if you caught
Carstairs on a rustling deal I say we'll string him up
here and now."

There was a stir at the door. The round-shouldered,
pot-bellied figure of Sheriff Lew Brady strode somewhat
unsteadily into the room. Drunk, Will Roman thought
tiredly.

Ignoring Engstrand, he said, "Brought you a customer,
Lew. Better get him locked away from this bunch. Henry
Freeman and I will prefer charges later."

Brady paused, blearily becoming aware of the air of
contention that existed between Sam Engstrand and
Will. It took him a long time to discover his keys, and
longer still to focus upon the man behind Roman. He
lumbered forward then, grinning as he sought to fit key
to the iron barred corridor door.

"Carstairs, eh? Well, I'll be hanged!" Brady guffawed.
"But I reckon it's more likely you that'll be hanged, eh,
Carstairs? Didn't know you was in the country. Thought
you'd lit out for good this last time. Bad business, boy,
runnin' out on your missus and the little tyke that way.
Well—"

"All right, Lew!" Roman snapped it off. The office of
sheriff had been created just three months ago, and in
Will's opinion Brady was the poorest choice of a lawman the community could have made. Brady's election
had started out as a joke among his cronies on Box and,
with typical cow country humor, the majority of the
punchers in the basin had joined in, voting the fat man
into office as a hoax which betrayed their own contempt
for the forces of law and order. Brady had been an in-
competent hand and Roman had been on the verge of
letting him go when the election came up.

"Sure. Sure, Will." Brady curbed his garrulous ram-
blings as the corridor door swung open beneath his hand.
"Far as I'm concerned Carstairs is as good as hung. He'll
be here when you want him. Don't worry none about
that."

"Just a minute, Brady." Engstrand moved forward deliberately, facing Will in the center of the room. "I'm saying there ain't nobody going to be locked up until we find out what this's all about. I'm warnin' you, Roman —the rest of us ranchers have got just as much say about what goes on in this basin as Box. You may have old man Fowler behind you, but in this country you're only a ramrod, mister, and you'd better not forget it. Understand?"

Will Roman drew a deep breath against the solid weight of fatigue that oppressed his body. Arriving in town, he had hoped that Engstrand and the Kesslers were still out continuing their three-day search of the hill country to the west of the basin. Well, he hadn't been so lucky. Or was it young Carstairs whose luck had run out?

Exhaling abruptly, he said, "All right, Sam. No need to get on your high horse. We came across Jack above Frenchman's Creek. He had a little bunch gathered and from where I sat I figured he was running them west toward the Gap." He shook his head at Engstrand's angry expression. "We ran him down a mile up the Creek," he added. "Every head in the bunch was wearing the Boxed F brand. It's not your affair, Sam. Jack's going into Miles for trial."

"Not my affair?" Engstrand swung around, demanding support from those behind him. "You hear that, gents? Nearly two hundred head I've lost this season alone, and he says it's not my affair! I start this little skunk hunt. I get all the boys together—but now it's not my affair!" He swung back savagely to face Will. "Well I say it is my affair and I aim to do something about it. Understand that, mister ramrod?"

With that, Engstrand started after Carstairs, who had ducked down the corridor. Carstairs took refuge behind Lew Brady as the sheriff struggled clumsily to unlock an empty cell door.

"Sam."

Roman's voice was not loud, but something in its tone seemed to hold Engstrand at the head of the corridor between the cells. Will unbuttoned his heavy coat, revealing the dark grip of the pistol holstered low on his thigh.

"Sam," he repeated, "I wouldn't start anything I couldn't finish, if I were you. Carstairs is going down to Miles in the morning. And he'll be in shape to ride. I hope I'll be able to say the same about you."

Silence crowded the room, broken only by inquiring calls from the street outside. Will Roman sighed. He had feared that something like this would happen. Henry Freeman and Amos Flushing had agreed readily enough to bring Carstairs in alive, they having no more taste for lynching than Roman himself. But Will had known Sam Engstrand would demand the rope for Carstairs the minute he discovered the facts. He could be thankful that he had seen no sign of Sam's three grown sons, or either of the Kessler brothers in the crowd outside— evidently Engstrand's groups had arrived in town some time ago and the others had already returned to their respective ranches—but this was quite bad enough. Carefully watching Engstrand's eyes, Will waited. At last Engstrand's nerve broke. He stomped back through the room toward the front door.

Men stepped aside to clear the path for Sam Engstrand. In the open doorway he turned, his massive, coarse features livid with fury.

"You've been ridin' high and mighty here on the Judith these past three years, Roman. But don't think you're too big to be pulled down. Carstairs is going to hang, understand? Me and my boys will see to that, and no two-bit foreman of Box is going to stop it."

The big man's gaze swung challengingly about the circle of faces nearest him. Will saw one or two of the townsmen push unconsciously back against those behind. When he spoke again, Engstrand's voice took on a deeper note of contempt and cunning.

"And another thing, mister: don't think the whole country won't figure out why the foreman of Box made such a point out of bringing Carstairs in alive when he should have been strung up on the spot. Men have eyes and ears in their heads whether you know it or not, sonny boy!"

Roman, who until now had felt only relief that the man

was leaving without creating an even greater issue between them, abruptly had an empty feeling in the pit of his stomach. Only dimly was he aware of the clanging of steel on steel and the tread of Brady's footsteps coming up toward the office.

"Sam," he said softly, "don't say anything you won't be able to take back."

Engstrand's laughter was harsh. His words carried clearly to those on the walk outside as well as to the dozen or so who had crowded into the office.

"Maybe you should have strung him up yourself, Roman. At least that would have given you a clear road with one rustler's wife."

Will Roman stood speechless. For well over a year he had tried to avoid an open break between himself, as representative of the largest spread on the Judith, and this man who, with his three grown sons, owned and operated the next most important ranch in the basin. Until now he had managed to ignore the personal level upon which Engstrand, as well as his oldest son, Jere, insisted upon stating their differences with the foreman of Ben Fowler's Boxed F. But in this moment, as he thought of Laurie Carstairs and the public slur Sam Engstrand had just cast upon her reputation, Roman threw aside all sense of responsibility to both his employer and the general welfare of the basin as a whole.

He said, "Sam, I thought you were old enough to know better. Seeing that you don't, I guess I'll have to teach you."

Roman moved forward. Sam Engstrand's eyes went wild. He cursed hoarsely, ripped off his coat and charged, huge arms flailing as he bore down on Will. Though the two were almost of a height, Engstrand's heavily muscled frame outweighed Roman .by at least thirty pounds. Meeting the man's charge, Will stepped in quickly, turning aside at the last instant to drive a short, chopping blow into Sam's ear. One of Engstrand's huge fists caught Will on the cheek. He ducked another and spun about behind the big man. He grasped Sam's belt at the small of his back and swung the rancher around. Then lifting his booted foot he shoved the man sprawling through the open doorway and onto the walk outside.

Engstrand bellowed and rolled into a forest of booted legs. Will followed him. Sam heaved himself up. Will hit him with the full force of his shoulder behind the blow, driving the big man once more into the human ring at his back. Blood flowed from the rancher's nose and mouth as he came forward once more.

Will tried a feint with his left. It didn't work. He took a solid, smashing blow on the side of the head that stunned him. A great, sledgelike fist took him again and light exploded before his eyes as he felt himself fall. He was not aware that he had fallen completely off the walk into the street's soft mud until he heard the crowd's yell and saw Engstrand's booted feet coming down upon him from the walk above.

Rolling aside, he heard Engstrand grunt as mud splattered from the impact of his landing. Will bunched his legs beneath him. He drove forward and up, taking Sam in the belly with the top of his head, clutching Sam about the waist as he continued to drive the man back. The rancher went down. Will rolled free and sent a roundhouse blow into Engstrand's battered face.

Once more on his feet, he had time for a single deep breath before Engstrand struggled up from the mud. Reaching forward, he grasped Engstrand's shock of hair in both hands. Using Engstrand's own forward drive as impetus, he braced himself abruptly so that the rancher was swung fully about by the hair of his head. At the end of the circle Roman drove his knee upward into Sam Engstrand's face.

Sam Engstrand straightened, confused and bellowing. Will hit him again. Blow by blow he drove Engstrand back and down. Bleeding, mud-encrusted, Sam Engstrand fell, struggled to rise, and fell again. Without knowing what he was doing, Roman bent and attempted to lift the man in order to strike him again. Hands clutched at his upraised arm and finally, Dusty's voice penetrated the fog that veiled his mind. He released his hold and allowed Engstrand's limp body to fall face down in the mud.

Twenty minutes later, sitting in the soapy, steaming water of the tub in the small back room of Art Lincoln's barber shop and tonsorial parlor—which was, incidentally, Judith City's latest and most civilized business venture to date—Will Roman tried to relax and let the water's soothing heat ease his mind as well as the tired and aching muscles of his body. But the effort was useless. He could not avoid the seriousness of the complications that were sure to arise as a result of an open break between Engstrand's Rocking Chair spread and Ben Fowler's Boxed F.

Had Will been able to keep his differences with Engstrand upon a purely personal plane, he would not have given the matter a second thought. But knowing the big rancher as he did, he realized that the stakes went far beyond any personal issue. Engstrand would not bother to muster support among the other ranchers of the basin merely to depose Will Roman as foreman of old Ben's Montana spread. For nearly a year now Roman had felt the antagonism of the Engstrands—particularly Sam and his eldest son, Jere—as a subtle force that was being directed against the welfare of the Boxed F itself.

Roman had known the Engstrand family down in Texas, long before the first combined drive northward onto Montana grass three years ago. Sam Engstrand had run a middling-fair spread across the river from Ben Fowler's home ranch on the Pecos. The summer Ben had sent Will, Dusty and Reno Sinclair north to scout the high border country with an eye to future graze, Engstrand and his two oldest sons had come along. The next year, when Ben sent nearly six thousand head north, Engstrand pulled up stakes, leaving Texas for good and joining his own two thousand head—all he owned—in with the Boxed F drive.

Roman had never liked the man, nor had he got along well with any of the family—with the possible exception of the youngest son, Mark. Immediately upon arrival in the basin of the Judith, and throughout the first and second winters, Engstrand had made infinite and overbearing demands upon Box in order to survive. Nor had the rancher taken what help Roman, at Ben Fowler's express order, had given him with any reaction but that of endless complaint and renewed demands upon Box's greater wealth and strength.

During the past year, which had seen Chair and several smaller independents become largely or completely self-sufficient, Engstrand's attitude had consisted of decrying the number of Texas stock Ben had continued to pour into the high border country each year. In the meantime, Roman knew, Sam Engstrand's hold had more than doubled. The man was well on his way to solid wealth—and without considering himself in any way, morally or otherwise, indebted to Box.

Of course, the rustling which had increased alarmingly during the past year was entirely a different matter. Even now, as he sought with damp hands to roll himself a smoke over the edge of the metal tub, Will could not bring himself to believe that Sam or his sons would actually deal in stolen stock. Jere Engstrand was a handy man with an iron when it came to marking an occasional unbranded calf, but gathering and running off stock that was ready for market. . . . No, even now, Roman didn't believe it.

He managed to get a dampish but smokable cigarette rolled, and was fumbling in the pockets of his muddy trousers for a match, when the flimsy door flapped open and Dusty Wilson stepped into the room. Will hunched his shoulders against the draft. The little tophand grinned.

"Be damned lucky if the only thing you catch is a cold," Dusty said, and laid a folded stack of clothing on the narrow bench against one wall. Striking a match, he leaned forward while Will dragged his smoke alight. "This was one night's work that's liable to pay off in lead nickels before we're through."

Roman's grin was wry. "Sounds like you're the one with a chill, son."

Dusty shook his head, rolling himself a smoke as he eased onto the beach. Though he was hardly a year younger than Will, the little tophand combined smoothly rounded features with a boyish mass of freckles above the line of a three-day growth of reddish blond beard, to present the appearance of a youth barely out of his teens. The silky, almost invisible texture of his lashes and brows added to the impression of open-faced innocence. These, plus the unprepossessing height of five-foot-six, had led many a larger man into the highly painful error of judging Dusty Wilson's temper and physical prowess by stature alone.

"Maybe I got me a chill and maybe I ain't," Dusty said. "All I'm saying is, I don't know if one yellow-back coyote like Carstairs is worth the fuss."

Roman flipped his waterlogged cigarette against the door, climbed out of the tub and began rubbing himself down with the towel Dusty handed him.

He said, "Carstairs had nothing to do with it."

"Yeah, I know." Dusty nodded. "I heard what Sam said. But it don't make a damn bit of difference when you add it all up. If we hadn't brought Jack in—"

Bent to towel his legs, Roman glanced up, the sudden intensity of his gaze cutting off Dusty's words. Yet even as he felt his anger rise, Will knew that Dusty was right. And so, in a way, had been Sam. For the hundredth time since they had run Jack Carstairs to earth that afternoon Will Roman found himself asking himself the same question: *Under the same conditions, would he have brought any other man back to face trial, rather than hang him on the spot?* Or, more definitely to the point: *Any man other than Laurie Carstairs' husband?*

But there was no profit in such speculation. He couldn't admit. . . .

Admit what?

With swift, impatient movements he thrust himself into the new clothes Dusty had picked up at Newton's store.

Damn it, of course there was no doubt about why he had brought Jack in. Not because of Carstairs' own worthless hide. A blind man could see better than that. Laurie Carstairs deserved a break. And yet, had he really given Laurie a break by bringing Jack in? Or had he only added to Laurie's burden by bringing back the man who had deserted her and her child last summer?

Buckling on his gunbelt, Will recalled that one moment when he'd had Jack Carstairs directly in his rifle's sights. *I don't know if one yellow-back coyote is worth the fuss,* Dusty had said. And Dusty was wrong a surprisingly small number of times. Well, the thing was done with now. But Sam . . . the words Sam Engstrand had used before the whole town. . . . "Hell," he muttered, and rolled his muddy clothes into a bundle to leave with Ruby Ferguson at the hotel. Giving a man a break because of his wife and kid was one thing. But the thing Sam Engstrand had hinted at—had openly stated, in fact—was a horse of a very different color.

Will yanked the door open. Dusty said mildly, "If you're figuring on declaring war on the whole human race you can count me out. Me, I'm for about twelve solid hours in the hay."

All at once, temper left Will Roman. This was not the first time Dusty had held a revealing mirror before him. He laughed and took a broad-handed swipe at the little tophand. Dusty nimbly avoided it and followed Roman into the shop up front.

Settling into the barber chair, Will said, "Tell Ruby I'll take the biggest steak she's got and don't spare the spuds." As Dusty moved toward the door Will turned his head beneath the lather-filled brush in the barber's hand, adding, "You'd better see that Lew's got Slim Olsen on the job. Whether Jack's worth the fuss or not, I didn't bring him into town to wind up in the hands of a lynch mob. Savvy, amigo?"

"Yeah, I savvy," Dusty said, and took off.

Will Roman settled down comfortably while Art Lincoln cautiously applied a steaming towel to his bruised and swollen face. He did not realize he had fallen asleep beneath the barber's sharp razor and gently professional touch until he was jarred awake by a gunshot outside.

In the instant before he came up from the chair, hardly aware of the precise little barber's headlong rush toward the door at the rear. Will heard the sloshing beat of hoofs and a high, ranting yell. His own weapon came to hand. He threw the haircloth aside and ran to the door. Down the street, coming on at a run, several riders were blasting the night's stillness with sixguns.

CHAPTER II

Will Roman's first reaction to the oncoming horde was a swift fear for the safety of the solitary prisoner in the jail across the street. He had stepped to the edge of the walk, seeing men duck back into the buildings along the street, when the broken, whooping yell of the foremost rider lifted again above the sound of guns. Recognition came then, and from the corner of his eye he saw Dusty Wilson, who had stepped out of the hotel farther on, shake his head as he slowly returned his sixgun to its holster. Roman followed suit, chuckling as he watched Reno Sinclair, followed by five or six Boxed F punchers, sweep past the hotel with a yipping burst of Indian yells and a renewed salute of sky-firing guns.

In front of Patterson's saloon, Sinclair set the bit against his horse's mouth. The animal braked to a halt as if it had hit a stone wall, rearing and pawing air as its rider came up in the stirrups, firing his last shots high in the air. Reno Sinclair might have a callous contempt for good horseflesh, as well as a deep-seated love of showmanship, but Reno Sinclair was in his glory at this moment.

He was a big man, Sinclair, an inch or more taller than Roman's six feet. His pale, blond, almost white hair curled upon his forehead as he batted a handsome Stetson against his mount's rump, circling through the group to come up to the rack before the saloon. His features were broadly handsome, and his clothing, from expensive hand-sewn boots to his knotted cravat and dark frock-coated suit, was fancy and fitted him to perfection. On impulse, as the swirl of riders drew up to the rack across

17

the street, Roman lifted his gun and sent a shot slamming skyward.

"All right, gents!" he shouted across the way. "If you've had your fun you can turn those guns in at the sheriff's office! We've got a jail here for the likes of you!"

As one the line of riders, some of them half out of the saddle, swung around, searching for the man who had spoken. Reno was the first to pull away, crossing the street to draw up at the rack in front of the barber shop.
· Scowling, he drawled elaborately, "Mister, ain't no cowtown sheriff north o' the Pecos can draw down on me an' my boys 'thout gittin' himself in trouble. Me, now, I just reckon I'm goin' to make you eat them words!"

With a strident whoop the big blond came down from the saddle. He splashed through the mud, jumped up to the walk and threw his arms around Roman. Laughing as he broke away, he hit Will solidly on the chest, and for a while they scuffled on the walk.

"Boy, you're a sight, and that's the damned truth," Sinclair said at last, gripping Will's hand. When Dusty come up and whispered to Will, "Need any help with this saddlebum, boss?" Reno roared again and swung at the little man. His blow missing by a good six inches. Dusty stepped in and neatly lifted Sinclair's pistol from its holster. Reno cursed.

"Damn you, Dusty boy! Some day you're going to get yourself shot pulling that little stunt. And I hope I'm there to see it, by hell!"

"Shot?" Dusty's innocently youthful features appeared even more boyish than usual as he appealed to Will. "Shot? What's the man mean, boss? Half shot, now, I could go for a little of that. But—"

Reno grabbed him, and the brief tussle ended in guffaws as Sinclair finally retrieved his gun. This was the way it always had been among Reno and Dusty and Will. Reno was the laughing, the careless one who had sparked their humor since they had ridden back to Texas after the War, eight years ago. Will Roman, who had grown to manhood on the Texas Box, had brought his two buddies back with him to take jobs with old Ben.

Now, *after three months in Texas, Reno had returned
once more to the Judith.

As they moved down the walk toward Ed and Ruby
Ferguson's Judith City Hotel and Saloon, Will caught
the sound of further hoofbeats and heard a man call out
from the livery stable at the head of the street.

"It's Ben! It's the old man hisself come to town!"

During the past few minutes, since Reno's flamboyant
entry had sent them scampering for cover, the citizens
had crowded once more out upon the walks. More than
a few had headed for the barber shop to greet Sinclair
and his bunch, who were well known to nearly everyone
in town. Now, however, as the new group of arrivals
swung more sedately up the street past Jess Logan's
stable, men stopped where they were. A slow-building
but enthusiastic clamor of welcome greeted the three
riders, most of it directed at the stout, upright, elderly
rancher whose Stetson was white as the horse he rode.

Ben Fowler lifted his hand in a friendly gesture as he
moved past Smith's Hardware, Newton's Mercantile and
Patterson's saloon. Men hurried along the walks as old
Ben Fowler and his two companions reined up before the
hotel where the Boxed F crew awaited him. Minutes later
Roman found himself standing at Ed Ferguson's bar between his employer and Reno, with Dusty beyond, and
the saloon rapidly filled to capacity as men pushed in
from the street and the entrance to the hotel's lobby at
one side of the room.

Smiling broadly, Ben Fowler had to raise his voice to
make himself heard. He was a chunky and somewhat
portly man in his early sixties with a massive, leonine
mane of pure white hair and bushy brows that jutted
belligerently above deep-set eyes of the sharpest blue.

He was a squareshooting and simple man, Ben Fowler,
and the patron and friend of every man on the Judith.
His had been the initiative and the expense and the risk
which had opened this far northern range. His had been
the dream and the vision, while the profits were shared
by all. Not only had Ben driven his vast herds north out
of Texas against the advice of supposedly wiser men, but
he had put up the money and cattle which helped to

establish several smaller ranchers on free Montana grass. He was a respected, beloved man in the eyes of the Judith ranchers and, though he preferred to live out his life on the home ranch in Texas, this night the Judith was his.

"Gentlemen," the old man said, "I give you a toast." Lifting his glass in salute, Ben turned to the three younger men who ranged the bar at his side, and Roman, sensing his intent, felt uneasy. "Gents, I give you the Boxed F ranch—the Montana Box—and the three men who located her, nursed her along and built her into what she is today. I give you Roman, Sinclair and Wilson. My boys, gents, and the rangiest, rootin' cowmen this side of the Pecos! To Box, gentlemen! Drink hearty!"

Red of face, Will caught Dusty's painfully embarrassed glance in the mirror behind the bar. Reno Sinclair laughed, draining his glass at a gulp.

Ten more minutes passed, with a continual line of townsmen, punchers and small ranchers pushing up to claim the privilege of shaking the old man's hand, before Ben nodded for Will to follow him into the hotel lobby.

"Well, son," Ben Fowler said, "two years is a right long spell for a pair of old rannahans like us to be ridin' different grass. This, now, this is good. Damned if it don't seem like the old days, sure enough."

Roman smiled, feeling a solid affection for the old man. Ben Fowler was more than merely Will's employer. He was practically the only father Roman had ever known. Ben and Amantha Fowler had adopted both Will Roman and Ellen Dunbridge when their families had been wiped out during the Mexican troubles, long before the War Between the States. Will had grown up on the Texas Box, and so had Ellen, four years the younger. At nineteen Will had gone off to war, bringing Reno and Dusty home with him when the fighting was done.

Biting the end from a fresh cigar, Ben said, "Ma and Ellen will be getting in some time tomorrow, providing that two-bit stage holds together between Miles City and here. Ma insisted on bringing so danged much folderol that Wakeley'll be lucky to get that team of his over the

Gap. Me, I couldn't wait for no stage with the smell of the Judith so close."

Roman contemplated telling Ben about Carstairs and the run-in with Sam Engstrand, but decided to let it go for the moment. Ben Fowler peered at Will from beneath his bushy white brows.

"How you taking it, son?" he asked suddenly. "How you taking this marriage of Ellen's and Reno's? Won't be no misunderstanding between you and Reno over it, will there?"

Roman had known that the question would come; in fact, he had prepared himself for it. Yet now that it was out, he felt a brief slice of the pain that had driven itself into his being when he received Ellen's letter a month ago. The same pain had overtaken him earlier this day when he recognized Reno on the street. He had thrust it aside then, and now he managed it again. His shrug was a casual gesture.

"What's there to misunderstand? She picked Reno herself, didn't she? Any man who didn't jump at the chance to marry Ellen would be a damned fool."

For a minute the old man remained silent, puffing thoughtfully on his cigar and studying the bare boards of the floor at his feet.

"Well," he said finally, "things is sure turning out a hell of a lot different than I figured they would. The day Bert Dunbridge died I promised myself I'd raise his daughter just like she was my own. Same as I did with you, son. Every year I've seen to it that the increase in old Bert's stock was tallied and marked with his Slash D brand. I reckon you know Ellen's a pretty wealthy young lady. With the last bunch I sent north to you, there's over five thousand head of her stock on Montana grass."

Roman knew all this. Ben Fowler had said it all before. Roman wondered what lay behind the old-timer's dust of words. But Fowler went on.

"That's a lot of beef, boy. Five thousand head—every last bit of old Bert's stock. I argued with the girl, told her she should leave at least half her tally on Texas grass. But she was too set on putting all her eggs in one basket." He paused, then added softly, "I'd hate to see it all get smashed at onct."

Will Roman at last understood the motive behind the old man's hedging. He shook his head tiredly, forcing a smile.

"Hell, you sound like Dusty, Ben. You know Reno. Full of hell and maybe a little free with liquor and cards. But he knows cattle and I've never seen him run from hard work."

"Yes, I know Reno," Ben Fowler agreed, but did not return the smile. "I know Reno and I'll tell you this right out—I don't like this wedding. I don't like it a bit. And that's aside from the fact that Ellen could have had you if she'd had any sense. Sure, Reno's a good enough hand. Might even make a good enough foreman, in a pinch. But with the responsibility and leeway of running his own spread—one he didn't have to work for—himself." Ben shrugged, but added, "You know damned well Reno's never saved a cent in all these years. You've taken out over half your pay in stock and Dusty's done the same, ever since you brought him down home after the war. But not Reno."

Will's fatigue deepened. This discussion was so useless. Ellen had married Reno a month ago—almost on the same day he had received her letter. The thing was over and done. What good could come from worrying over it now like some dog over a meatless bone? Yet even before the old rancher spoke again Roman realized that Ben had gone beyond mere worry. Old Ben's hard-clenching jaw told Will that he had something definite in mind.

"No, not Reno," Fowler repeated softly. "And that's why I'm talking to you now, son. That's why I've made up my mind to ask you the favor I've got to ask."

Will held his silence. As far as he was concerned it was the old man's show.

"Will." Fowler's voice stiffened with final decision. "I want you to let Dusty go."

Roman stared at him. Fowler hurried on.

"I know, I know. Dusty's your own right hand. He's as important to you as you are to me—and I couldn't get along five minutes without you. But I'm still asking you to let him go. I want him on Ellen's place—Reno's place, if that's the way it's got to be. That's the least amount of insurance I can give old Bert's girl now. The least, and for all I know, the most." He lifted a hand to Will's shoulder, looking him squarely in the eye.

"Maybe it don't seem fair to you—Reno getting your *segundo* as well as your girl—but that's the way I want it, Will. There's a lot of things in this life, son, that ain't exactly what you might call fair."

A sudden, bitter sense of hopelessness and futility built up in Will Roman, fed by the deep well of his own fatigue. He was tired, exhausted, and in far more than body alone. What could he say? Glancing up, he saw Ruby Ferguson in the dining room doorway and realized he had not eaten since morning. The thought came that he should tell Ben about Carstairs and Engstrand, but he realized he was in no mood to go into the matter now.

He said, "Sure, Ben. I see what you mean. Right now I'm for a little grub and a few hours' sleep. Dusty and I have been in the saddle the last three days and nights. I've got a few other things to go over with you, but I reckon they'll wait till morning."

"Sure, son, sure." Ben nodded, cocking an ear at the saloon where the hubbub of merriment continued unabated. "I'll be staying over tonight and we'll ride out to the place together first thing tomorrow."

As the elderly rancher moved back into the barroom Roman crossed to the dining room at the rear of the lobby. Ruby Ferguson, a stout but attractive woman in her early thirties, gestured toward a table near the kitchen. When he had let himself into a chair she stood a further moment, studying the deep lines of fatigue in his face and the slight swelling of one cheek that Engstrand's fist had caused.

"You drive yourself too hard," she said, genuinely concerned. "Some day you'll find out that one man alone can only do so much and no more."

Will grinned. "No sermons, Ruby. Food. Food and I'm going to drive myself to sleep. I think I'm good for that much more."

She left him, returning shortly with a huge platter of

steak, fried eggs and potatoes. She brought coffee and poured it steaming into his cup. She was a woman who had once been more than merely attractive, Roman knew, though the years had taken their toll. Ed, her husband, somehow had never managed to make a success of ranching. Will himself had suggested their opening the hotel in Judith City the year before and upon his recommendation Ben had financed the venture, taking over the Fergusons' small spread as partial payment. Ed, a skinny and prematurely balding man, ran the barroom while Ruby cooked, waited table and took care of the rooms upstairs. Watching Will now as he ate, Ruby wore an expression that was a mixture of maternal regard and something far more femininely personal.

She said, "You're liable to pay a pretty big price for bringing Jack in. You know that, don't you, Will?" At his look she added quickly, "I know. It's none of my damned business. But I hate to see you take a beating for the sake of a miserable little coward who's not worth the powder and lead to blow him to hell."

"It's all right, Ruby. I think Box will survive."

"Box might. But will you?" She tucked several loose tendrils of hair into place in the rolled bun at her neck. She said, "After that beating you gave Sam tonight he and his boys will be after your hide and you know it. And another thing: if I were you I'd keep my eye on Frank and Dobe Kessler. From here on out Sam is not going to be too particular what kind of company he keeps. And I've smelled prettier skunks in my time than those two Kessler boys."

When Ruby returned to the kitchen, Will tried to give due consideration to her warning, but found that he could muster little concern over Sam Engstrand or the Kessler brothers. Drinking his coffee, he mulled over Ben's news about Ma Fowler and Ellen. Ellen Dunbridge. Ellen Dunbridge Sinclair. . . . With surly impatience he kicked back his chair and strode toward the lobby.

All right! She married Reno didn't she? The wash of a sudden anger swept beyond control. He told himself viciously, *You sent him south every year instead of going yourself, didn't you? What the hell did you expect? Did you think she would wait all her life?*

Clumping toward the stairs, Will Roman felt a brief compulsion to drink himself into a stupor. He listened to the uproar in the barroom and fought down the impulse. He had mounted the first few steps when the street door opened and a feminine voice called his name. Turning, he saw a young woman in a worn yellow slicker standing inside the small lobby. In this first instant of surprise he did not notice the heavy pistol she held extended downward at her side.

"Laurie. What—"

"You'll not do it, Will Roman!" He walked slowly back down the steps and started across the lobby. The gun came up in her hand, centering on his chest.

"You'll not do it," she repeated. "Not you nor any of the others. No matter what anyone might think of Jack, he's my husband and I'll not stand aside and watch him hang."

And then, as if Laurie Carstairs had given a signal, the slapping reverberation of gunfire broke out in the street. Roman stiffened. The babble of voices from the adjoining saloon died out. One final shot exploded over the town, followed by the muffled, sloshing sound of running hoofs in the street's wet mud.

"They got Lew's deputy!" someone outside shouted. "They shot Slim Olsen! Carstairs is getting away!"

CHAPTER III

The rush of the crowd from barroom to street came like a stampede. Will dashed past Laurie Carstairs and through the open door at her back. From the walk outside he had a fleeting glimpse of a single rider as man and horse disappeared into the darkness beyond Logan's stable. The crowd rolled out then, spilling over the walk and into the street in front of the hotel's saloon.

"There was two of 'em! I seen the whole thing!" A man ran up the walk toward the crowd, shouting breathlessly. "They busted Carstairs out and shot Olsen down in cold blood!"

Dusty moved up the walk to stand at Will's side.

"Well, boy," the little tophand said, "it looks like we pulled a bigger minnow out of the creek than we figured when we brought Jack in. From where I'm standin' I'd say at least a couple other fishermen were downright jealous of our catch."

In front of the saloon the man who had claimed he had seen the whole thing was being questioned by the crowd. Seeing Ben Fowler and Reno Sinclair in the midst of the group, Roman nodded at Dusty.

"I'd say this fishing party was just getting its second wind." He paused, making a rapid decision as the growling demands for the formation of a general posse arose from the crowd. He talked fast, telling Dusty to bring two fresh mounts around to the hotel's back door as quickly as possible. As Dusty hurried off toward Logan's stable Roman stepped back into the lobby.

Laurie Carstairs, eyes wide, stood in the protective circle of Ruby Ferguson's arms. She still held the revolver

26

with which she had threatened him, but her arm hung
limply at her side, the weapon forgotten.

"Did—did they kill him? Oh, Will, did they—"

She came forward then, leaving Ruby to throw herself
against him. The pistol clattered to the bare board floor
as she buried her head against his chest.

"No. No, he got away, Laurie. But this time it looks
pretty bad." He held her gently, reaching up to remove
the oilskin rainhat that was twisted askew upon the soft,
burnished gold of her hair. He glanced at Ruby, tossing
his head in a brief warning gesture at the open door and
the street at his back. As he led Laurie toward the dining
room and the kitchen, Ruby Ferguson closed the front
door. She bent to retrieve the pistol Laurie had carried,
paused for a glimpse into the deserted saloon, then followed the pair across the small lobby.

Laurie Carstairs was a tall slender girl, not more than
twenty-two or -three, with ash-blonde hair and clear gray
eyes that looked directly at a person when she spoke.
Now, seated across the table from the girl in Ruby Ferguson's kitchen, Will Roman appreciated more than ever
the unhappiness and insecurity which had been Laurie's
lot. As the girl sipped thankfully at the hot coffee Ruby
placed before her, Will noticed the worn Levis and faded
shirt she wore and realized he had never seen Laurie in
proper woman's dress.

The Carstairs' had come north with the Boxed F's
second drive out of Texas two years ago. Jack Carstairs
had never been fitted for the responsibilities of either
marriage or parenthood. A footloose puncher, he had married Laurie in a small town in eastern Texas. Will knew
Laurie's father had provided the money for the few
miserable head Jack had driven north for a start on Montana grass. But the going had been too tough, the life too
rigid for Jack. He had taken to gambling and liquor and,
when there was no money for either, had taken to riding
the hills for weeks at a time, leaving his wife and infant
son to shift for themselves in the small cabin on Alder
Creek. Since early summer he had disappeared, though
the nature of his activities during these past months had
been fully clarified today.

Roman understood the helplessness and fear that had clouded Laurie's eyes and twisted her mouth when she stared at him after the shooting upon the street. Often during past months he had urged her to return to her father's home in Texas, but she had stoutly refused. Less than two weeks ago, when he offered to buy what few head of cattle Jack had not already sold, she had revealed the fact of her father's death. And tonight, though it had been a futile gesture, and born of sheer desperation, she had come to rescue her husband, sixgun in hand.

Suddenly Will felt bitterly jealous of this worthless man who could inspire such devotion from a woman like Laurie. In spite of himself, a comparison between this girl and Ellen stirred through the screen of his mind. If Jack was making good his escape in this moment, Roman knew that Laurie had had no hand in the affair. He recalled again that moment this afternoon when he'd had Carstairs framed in his sights, and realized now the fool he had been to hold his fire.

"It's all right," he said finally. "It may be the best thing all around if he gets away."

"But—but where will he go? What will he do? And who are *they*, Will? Who would help Jack escape?"

"Worrying about it will do no good." Ruby spoke briskly as she bustled about the stove, fixing the girl a meal. "And it's too late for you to ride back tonight. You get a good night's sleep here. You left someone with the boy?"

Laurie nodded. "I left him with Mrs. Flushing before I came into town." She looked at Will with renewed anxiety. "They'll hunt him down. They'll hunt him down like a mountain cat. Oh, Will—" tears gathered suddenly in her eyes—"could you—"

"I'll do what I can." Drinking the last of his coffee, Will came to his feet as the back door opened and Dusty Wilson stepped quietly inside. Roman avoided the girl's gaze, forcing himself to withhold the words of reassurance his compassion urged him to give. He said, "I'm afraid Jack's gone a little too far this time, Laurie. We don't know if the men who busted him out are his friends or his enemies. But in either case—" he shook his head

quickly— "it might be a good idea to prepare yourself
for whatever might come."

Laurie raised her fingers to a blue vein that throbbed
in the white column of her throat.

"I'm sorry, Will. I acted like such a fool, riding in with
a gun that way. I—I guess I must have been out of my
mind." The futile, pathetic little smile she gave him
sliced into Will like a blade. "I'll be all right. I know
you'll do what you can."

Roman glanced at Ruby. She winked reassuringly and
he stepped through the back door behind Dusty. Two
horses stood beside the outside staircase that ran up to
the second floor behind the hotel.

"Lew's making up a posse." Dusty snorted, indicating
his opinion of Lew Brady's abilities as a lawman. "The
old man's all excited about it and swears he's going
along. Reno—" the little puncher's shrug was expressive
—"he's loaded for bear and rangy as a little dog at a pic-
nic. From what I picked up they'll head straight south
for the Gap. Reckon they figure Jack and his buddies are
headed out of the country."

Will said, "And what do you figure?"

"Me, I figure I'd like to get some sleep, but know
damned well I ain't. And I figure we better get outa here,
too, if we're going to play that hunch I see runnin' around
in your head. The old man will be collarin' us to trail
along with Lew's so-called posse, first thing you know."

Roman swung up to saddle, Dusty following suit.
As they rode off through the darkness Will said, "You
figure Jack's headed out of the country with a couple of
his buddies?"

"Friends?" Dusty said. "I never heard of Jack Carstairs
having any friends. But they's sure some critters around
what'd like to see him hangin' high to a tree."

They circled around the back edges of town and struck
the main road.

"I may be wrong on this, Dusty," Will said. "Rustling
is one thing, but killing Slim Olsen was murder. Yesterday I'd have said a man was crazy if he'd told me Sam
Engstrand was mixed up in this."

Dusty rode along in silence for a while. Then he said

slowly, "Well, it won't hurt to check. Offhand, I'd say someone was mighty interested in keeping Jack from talking. It could be Sam, or—" he shrugged—"it could be someone else." When Will did not speak he added softly, "It's round, square and even, though, that we'll come across Jack's body one of these days after the buzzards have had their fill."

Roman considered the problem, oblivious to the occasional patches of moonlight and darkness running across the land beneath high, scudding clouds. Though he felt sure that Lew Brady's posse, including Ben and Reno, would have their ride for nothing, he was not at all certain that his own present course would prove more effective. Sam Engstrand had sworn that he and his boys would see Carstairs hang. Yet in spite of this fact, doubt gnawed at Will's mind. He recalled Ruby Ferguson's warning about Frank and Dobe Kessler. Actually, what did he know of this pair? Dusty himself had said it looked like someone wanted to keep Jack from talking. Yet, if it had been the Kessler brothers—if they were mixed up in the rustling along with Jack—why had they not put a bullet into Carstairs there in the jail instead of killing another man in order to break him free?

Sam Engstrand's Rocking Chair headquarters was less than five miles from town. After they had covered half this distance and were swinging up the bank of a small creek, Roman drew in, whispering to Wilson. Halting beside a screening clump of second growth alder, they waited. The muffled thuds of hoofs upon the damp earth grew near. Roman eased his pistol from holster, and as the moon's light momentarily broke through the clouds overhead, he sent a crisp order toward the two mounted men who were revealed as they approached.

"That's far enough, boys. Hold it right there."

A man cursed, his mount snorting and rearing nervously against the bit. Roman identified the voice of Jere Engstrand, Sam's oldest son. He said, "No gunplay, Jere. You're plenty covered. That young Mark with you?" He thought he had recognized the younger Engstrand's whispered tones as he gentled his mount. But Jere Engstrand had no patience for questions.

"Damn it," he snarled, "this cuts it for sure! We're on Chair grass here! One of these days I'll—"

"You'll keep shut," Will Roman told him, "or it won't be one of these days. It'll be now." He reined forward, Dusty moving out at his side, toward the younger Engstrand. "Your pa home, Mark? And your brother Matt?"

"Keep shut, kid," Jere Engstrand said.

Roman said, "I'm not here because of what happened between your pa and me tonight, Mark. That was different and completely personal. Less than an hour ago two men shot Slim Olsen down and broke Carstairs out of jail."

Jere Engstrand exploded. "Broke Carstairs out? By heaven, Roman, this is your doing! Pa warned me you'd pull something like this! Just because you and that Carstairs woman—"

"Mister," Will Roman said, "I skinned my knuckles on one Engstrand tonight for not keeping a civil tongue in his head." He gestured to the man at his side. "Dusty, take our friend off a bit and let him cool down."

Wilson reined in, gun drawn. Jere hesitated, moving away with a last warning to his brother. The two men had gone but a few yards, however, when a cloud obscured the moon. The sudden, drumming beat of hoofs upon the sodden earth, joined with Dusty's raised shout, told Roman that Jere had bolted. He called to Wilson. Mark Engstrand made no move to escape and Dusty jogged back a moment later. It was so obvious that Dusty's only choice had been to let Jere go, or chance a shot that might prove fatal, that he didn't bother mentioning it. Will looked at Mark Engstrand.

"What about it, boy? You see we've got to get to the bottom of this, don't you? This wasn't a shooting. It was outright murder. I'll ask you again about your pa and Matt."

Mark Engstrand was barely twenty. As occasionally happens in families, his nature was almost the complete opposite of that of his father and two older brothers. He had been a shy and sensitive boy and had changed little with the passage of years. Back in Texas before the war, Mark, bullied by his brothers, often had sought

Will's company, spending almost as much time on Box as he had at home. Will himself had come to blows with both Jere and Matt over their treatment of their younger brother.

Now the boy seemed to hesitate. He fidgeted beneath Roman's stare, but finally answered.

"Hell, Will, I don't see why you had to beat Pa down like you did. You know how he is. He ain't going to forget it noways soon."

Roman held his impatience in check, knowing that Mark would go on. Mark sniffled and for a moment Will thought he might cry.

"You hurt him pretty bad," Mark said. "He got home about an hour ago and went right⋅ to bed. Matt's ridin' line up on Dog Creek Meadow. Pa, he told me and Jere to ride into town to make sure nothin' happened to Carstairs. Said he wanted to be damned sure Jack got what was comin' to him, one way or the other."

Roman knew the boy was telling the truth. He said, "All right, Mark. No need for you to ride in now, unless you want to hear what happened from some of the others in town. Brady's got up a posse, but I doubt if they'll find anything tonight." He turned to follow Dusty, who had started down toward the creek, but paused once more. "I'm sorry it had to happen, about your pa and me, Mark. But there are some things a man can't let go by."

Roman swung down across the swollen creek and up the far bank. After little more than an hour's steady riding he and Dusty reined into the yard at Box. China John was still up. He offered to cook them something to eat, but they refused. Informing the Oriental of the imminent arrival of Ben and Amantha Fowler and Ellen, Roman moved his things into the bunkhouse beside the barn. Dusty had moved into the bunkhouse when it was built, but Reno had stayed on in the log-walled ranch house with Will. Coming to the door of Reno's room with an armful of clothes, Roman halted.

Sinclair, of course, would be building his own headquarters as soon as things were settled. But the thought that this room, next to the one he had occupied for the better part of three years, would soon belong to Ellen

and Reno brought a sudden shock of realization home to
Will. With the toe of his boot he pushed the door open,
staring at the shadowy outlines of bed and dresser in the
light that came down the hall from the main room up
front. Ellen . . . Mrs. Ellen Sinclair.

There was no anger in him now, but a surge of rank
futility, amounting to an actual physical sickness, sent
him quickly along the hallway and out of the house.

Reno Sinclair swore as an unseen bough knocked his
hat awry, drenching him with its watery burden. He gave
spur to his mount, urging the animal on up the slope
through the pines. The moon's wan light pierced the timber only occasionally, being more of a hindrance than
help in his attempt to follow the none too familiar
trail.

Less than an hour before, Reno had taken his chance,
dropping back from the main body of Lew Brady's posse
to swing off the main road into the hills west of the Gap.
It had not been a smart maneuver, he knew. By the time
they reached the Gap Ben and the others would miss
him. But since the moment he had learned of Carstairs'
capture and subsequent escape, he had not been able to
contain his anxiety.

Several times in the next fifteen minutes he stopped,
trying to get his bearings by the moon's position and the
general contour of the country. At last, striking a long
narrow meadow through which a small stream wound
in reflected silvery light, he went across it and struck the
timbered slope at a more confident pace.

If only he'd not been such a damned fool this summer
before he rode south! As it turned out, he had not needed
the money at all. No, not *needed* it . . . but he had spent
it just the same, hadn't he? Dropped the bulk of it at
poker and faro at railhead in Laramie City before he had
got halfway to Texas! Yes, he'd been a fool all right; but
the money was the least of his worries now.

Carstairs, now: there was the danger. Good God! What
if it hadn't been Frank and Dobe at all? In town there
had been some talk about Engstrand and his intentions
concerning Jack. If Sam and his boys had broken Car-

stairs out . . . and if Jack had talked. . . . In spite of the
night's increasing cold, Reno broke into a sweat. Viciously
he roweled his animal's flanks, and ten minutes later he
crested a rise that gave onto a large mountain meadow
against the far side of which the lighted windows of a
log-walled house shone yellow beneath the moon's eerie
glow.

Stopping well short of the house, he cupped his hands
and called out above the racket of several yapping dogs.
The lighted windows went dark. He saw the door open
and heard a questioning voice. He answered and rode in,
dismounting before the door.

As light came up once more in the house, one of the
mongrel dogs charged, snapping. Reno caught the mutt
in the throat with a swift kick. Thrown sprawling across
the yard, the dog ran howling into the night. Reno
stepped inside.

"No need for that, Sinclair." Frank Kessler was a thin,
hump-shouldered man with a frown of disapproval
stamped upon a narrow face entirely dominated by his
high, beaked nose and small, peering black eyes. He
crossed the room, walking with a decided limp, one
shoulder held several inches higher than the other. A
second man, standing beside the open fireplace, laughed
harshly.

"Let him have his fun, Frank," Dobe Kessler said. "A
man ought to be able to kick somethin' around, even if
it's only a dog."

"One of these days," Reno told Dobe, "I may mistake
you for one of your curs."

Dobe Kessler came toward Reno. Though inches
shorter than Reno, he was a wide barrel-chested man
with thick arms and shoulders encased in a filthy woolen
undershirt which had lost all semblance of its original
color. One eye, which evidently had been pierced years
before, was a milky dark gray blur, accenting the pin-
point focus of its mate as he stared at Sinclair. Dobe appeared a good ten years younger than his brother; he
could have been anywhere between thirty and forty. He
tapped Reno on the chest with a thick, heavy finger.

"Any time, mister," he said. "Just any time at all."

Without warning, Reno's temper exploded. Whatever he might be, Reno Sinclair was no physical coward; and in this moment, with the gnawing uncertainty of the past several hours upon him, he felt nothing but an angry contempt for the man before him. The heel of his hand connected solidly with Dobe Kessler's square chin, sending Dobe back into a chair that tripped him. As Dobe went down, cursing, Reno's hand darted beneath the lapel of his long frock coat, coming out with the Colt he carried in a shoulder holster. The weapon's blued length glinted, dully in the lamplight, covering the man on the floor.

"I won't dirty my hands on you, Dobe. You come up off that floor, and I swear, I'll put a bullet through your brisket. Understand?"

Resting upon an elbow, Dobe looked up at Sinclair, his one good eye gleaming. He wiped a hand across his beard-stubbled chin, and he said, "Mister Fancy Pants Sinclair, eh? What'd I tell you, Frank? I told you the boy'd get big ideas once he laid hands on the Slash D hold." He snorted. "What about it, Reno? All signed, sealed and delivered, eh? Funny how big a marriage license can make some men feel."

Reno thumbed back the hammer of the Colt and let it drop. The jarring blast of the weapon filled the room. The bullet passed between Dobe's chest and the arm that propped him up, and splintered through the floor. Dobe's grin was wiped out as though it had never existed and for one fleeting instant genuine fear drained color from the man's heavy face.

"All right. All right, Sinclair." Frank Kessler's whine rose in protest. Frank was armed but he made no attempt to use his weapon. He hobbled over and prodded his brother with the toe of his boot. "You," he said. "Git up and act like you got some sense for a change. Ain't none of us goin' to get nowhere a-squabblin' and kickin' up a fuss like a bunch of snot-nosed kids."

Limping across to a table, he sat down and sloshed whisky from a quart bottle into a dirty tin cup. After a quick gulp he peered at Sinclair, wiping his whiskered mouth upon the filthy sleeve of his coat.

"That right, Sinclair?" he asked in his high whining
tone. "You got things all tied up? You and the Dunbridge
gal all hitched legal and fair?"

Reno could have stood a drink but he couldn't ask for
one. Holstering his weapon carefully, he stayed where
he was, keeping a wary eye on both Kesslers.

"That's neither here nor there and you damned well
know it," he said. "You know why I'm here. What about
this Carstairs thing?"

Rising, Dobe Kessler rounded his brother's chair,
reached for the bottle upon the table and took a drink
from its neck. Frank Kessler shook his head.

"Don't know about that bein' neither here nor there,
boy," he said dryly. "Far as Carstairs is concerned I'd
say you don't need to worry none about him. We can lay
hand on him when we like, and that's all that counts.
But you, now. Four, five thousand head of Slash stock.
Hell, you're a big man now, Sinclair. Dobe and me, we
like to do business with big men. Sort'a adds a little
prestige to things—eh, boy?"

After a second drink Dobe Kessler wheezed. Then he
laughed, but there was no humor in the sound.

"Hell yes, Frank. And I figure there ought to be a hell
of a lot more than prestige added to the next little deal
we have with Mister Fancy Pants Sinclair. A hell of a lot
more!" His good eye sharpened on Reno across the room.
"Say about five, maybe six hundred head, Mister
Sinclair?"

Reno's pulse pounded in sudden outrage. Once more
he cursed himself inwardly, realizing he might have
known how things would go. Attempting to hold his fury
in hand, he said stiffly, "You and Dobe figuring to blackmail me, Frank? You think because Jack knows about our
little deal last summer, you can hold him over my head?"

Dobe's snorting laugh was scornful, but the older Kessler cut him off with an upraised hand.

"Call it anything you like," Frank Kessler said. "Me, I
kind of figure we're makin' a trade. Me and Dobe, we
helped you out this summer when you figured to raise a
little extra coin. Now the boot's on the other foot. Carstairs? I'd say he's just me and Dobe's ace in the hole.

You play along with us and I reckon you won't have to worry none about Jack."

"And you'll play along with us! Understand that right now!" Dobe's voice lashed across the room. "That hundred head of Slash D stuff you sold us last summer ain't a drop in the bucket to the business we're goin' to do. And at our prices, not yours!" The stocky man rounded the table, sneering.

"Hell, you didn't think you could jump in and take what you wanted and jump out again, did you, Reno? Even Jack Carstairs ain't that dumb. You drove a hundred head of stock off Box grass and Carstairs can swear in court he helped you do it. Sure, he might get a light sentence. But for turnin' evidence on you it wouldn't be much. And where would you be then?"

Reno did not realize that he had moved toward Dobe until Frank Kessler's voice turned him. The butt of Frank's pistol rested upon the table, its muzzle pointing at Reno's stomach.

"Ain't no sense in losin' your temper," Frank whined. "Me and Dobe, now, we'd like to see a nice little bunch, say fifty head, show up in Dog Creek Meadow at least twice a month. And just to show you we ain't really down on you, it don't have to be Slash stock. Box, Chair, hell, any of the valley stuff. It's all the same to us."

Kessler got to his feet, gesturing toward the door with his gun. For an instant Reno judged his chances, then gave up the thought. Raging inwardly, he strode through the door and stepped up to his mount in the yard. Frank's voice followed him as he reined around before the door.

"You just take it easy, son, and you'll be all right. You and me and Dobe, hell, we'll get fat on this deal before we're through. Don't you worry none about that."

Spurring off across the meadow toward the dropping trail beyond, Reno heard Dobe Kessler's grating laughter rise to follow him.

CHAPTER IV

Rising early next morning, Will Roman finished his breakfast before Wilson and the four riders who were not on duty elsewhere trooped into the large kitchen at the back of the house. Of the four Box hands, two had ridden in from different line camps the day before. Lingering over extra coffee, Will discussed the various details concerning the disposition and condition of the several herds which were being moved onto winter graze in preparation for the coming, season. Beneath the punchers' chiding banter, China John kept a steady stream of griddle cakes, ham, eggs and fried potatoes moving between stove and table. Though he had lived in the country twenty years, the Oriental's singsong pidgin speech was a continual source of delight to most of the Boxed F hands.

Owing to the distance and length of time involved in reaching railhead at Laramie City, the general roundup, branding and selecting of salable stock had taken place earlier in the year. On his way south to Texas three months before, Reno had bossed a drive of fifteen hundred beeves to Laramie, this bunch representing the first actual sale of Boxed F stock since the Judith country had been opened to graze. Will knew, however, that it would be only a matter of time before the railroads would extend north and west into the high border country, thus eliminating much of the loss and work involved in each yearly drive. Already the Montana Box was completely independent of the home ranch down in Texas. It was a cattleman's paradise, this basin of the Judith.

Will Roman was well aware of his position on Box. Both Ben and Amantha Fowler, childless, had long looked

upon him as their own son. This, as they had regarded
Ellen Dunbridge as a daughter. From the moment Will
had sat beside Dusty in the Gap at the head of the
Judith Basin three years ago, he had known that the
ranch he was to build in this high northern country would
one day be his. He had known too of the dangers of
human avarice and greed, of the temptations to over-
graze, and of the many prejudices, both personal and
policy-wise, which must be overcome in the successful
establishment of a new community.

Yet now, as Roman left the others to finish their meal
and crossed the yard toward barn and corrals, he wondered if he—or any man—were capable of securing a
peaceful progress against the tide of conflict inherent in
such a community.

Establishment, growth, success: these things depended
upon the strength and purpose of the community as a
whole. Yet that overall purpose and strength was a chain
welded of individual links; and upon the validity, the
soundness, of each individual rested the welfare of all.
But could a man tear dishonesty from the mind of another, stifle jealousy, kill that greed which, combined with
suspicion and distrust, was perhaps the worst passion of
all? And what about Will Roman himself? Did a man,
filled with these same weaknesses and petty emotions, set
himself up to judge? To condemn?

Realizing that he had for some time been standing idle,
holding the corral gate ajar, Roman went inside, pulling
it to behind him. Halter in hand, he moved toward the
half dozen nervously footing horses across the enclosure.
Deep in his mind he knew he had been a fool in the matter of Carstairs. The man was a proven rustler and by
every moral code known to the cattleman he should have
been hanged on the spot. This was what hurt. The break
between Chair and Box would not have occurred had he
fulfilled the duties of his own position. And again he had
been a fool in suspecting Engstrand in the matter of
Jack's escape. This, because of his own groundless suspicion and distrust. *Good God, is no man immune?* In
bitterness, as he slipped the halter upon a roan gelding,

it came·to him that man's greater heritage was blindness, not trust.

He finished saddling the gelding. The crew came out. The pair who had ridden in yesterday had their orders, and they quickly saddled and rode away from the ranch. Dusty moved toward the barn to hitch up the rig that would bring Ellen and Amantha Fowler from town. Will called to Hank Crawford, one of the older hands who had ridden for Box since Roman himself was a boy.

"I want you to get your stuff together and ride over to the Carstairs place," he told Hank. "You can fix yourself up a bunk in the barn. I'd appreciate it if you'd give Mrs. Carstairs a hand till we see what's to be done. It's my guess she'll not be able to get through the winter alone."

Crawford brushed back the ends of his drooping mustache and spat cleanly across a patch of yard. It had been Will's hope, this past summer, that the valley would see fit to elect Hank Crawford as sheriff. He was a steady, reliable and clear-thinking man. But Hank himself, for reasons he did not care to state, had refused to run. Now he cocked one weathered brow at Will.

"Wondered how long you was goin' to let that little lass sit out there and starve herself plumb down to the ground." He paused, squinting up as the sun broke clear of the hills that lifted directly east of the ranch. "I figure you're right about her not makin' it this winter. But somethin' tells me Ruby and Ed could sure use some help at that hotel."

Roman smiled. "It's a good idea, Hank. We'll see. But I've got an idea it'll take some talking. You ride on over. And don't take no for an answer. *Sabe usted?*"

Without waiting for Dusty, Will stepped.to the saddle and rode out for town. Though he had intended to mention the matter of Ben's desires where the little tophand was concerned, he had not been able to bring himself to it, divining beforehand Dusty's reaction to such a plan. In spite of the friendship that had existed so long among Reno, Dusty and himself, Will knew that the past three years had wrought a subtle change.

During the years in Texas it had been share and share alike. But from the moment they had completed their first drive north it became apparent, at least to Will, that such was no longer the case. That Roman would assume command of the Montana Box was understood from the first. This Dusty had accepted as a matter of course. To Reno, however, it had been one thing to ride beside Will Roman on equal terms at the Texas Box, but quite another to work under him on the northern spread.

Reno's growing independence of manner, his preoccupation with matters other than the work in hand, had become obvious to both Dusty and Will. Sensing the injured pride in the man, Roman had persuaded Ben Fowler to appoint Reno trail boss on subsequent drives. Nor had Will's faith been displaced—at least so far as Reno's ability to handle the huge herds and the crews it took to drive them was concerned.

Reno was a good cattleman and a hard worker—when he thought he was getting his due. Yet for the past two years he had done little but rest on his laurels as a competent trail boss, idling his time and money away in Sid Patterson's saloon in between the three major drives he had brought out of Texas.

This behavior of Reno's had had more than a little effect on Dusty. And now, to ask Dusty to give up his job on Box and hire out to Reno on his new Slashed D spread. . . . No, Will Roman thought. Ben had badly misjudged the situation if he supposed either Dusty or Reno would tolerate such an arrangement.

As he forded the shallow river outside of town, Will reflected sourly that the old man was far from infallible. Of a generation who had taken what they wanted and held it by force, Ben Fowler was far too prone to paint men and situations alike with the sweeping stroke of a black or white brush. His faith in the one, and complete intolerance for the other, was too definite, too lacking in appreciation of the shadings of character and event Will himself beheld in the world. Ben had built his life upon yes or no, right or wrong, and by sheer force of insistence catalogued each man, each woman, each eventuality, into one square hole or the other. To Will, such decisive presumption was far too crude, and as he entered the town's single street, he could only hope that this di-

vergence of view would not one day find him opposed to
a fine old man who had always treated him as a son.

He had not expected to find the stagecoach already in
town. It had been his intention, in fact, to pause in Judith
City only long enough to ascertain whether Lew Brady's
posse had stumbled upon some lead before he continued
south to pay a belated visit upon the Kessler brothers.
Too, though he had not considered it consciously, he
realized now that he had secretly hoped neither Ben nor
Reno would be up and about after their long night's
ride. Ben, he knew, would have more than a few words
to say about the Carstairs deal as well as Will's squabble
with Sam Engstrand.

Yet now, at sight of the stage, which evidently had
arrived but minutes before, these other considerations
dropped away. Tom Wakeley, wide-hatted, heavily
bearded and wearing the weathered buckskins he likely
had been born in, was handing the first of a towering
cargo of suitcases, trunks and odd bundles down to Ed
Ferguson on the walk. Roman reined in and returned the
driver's boisterous greeting. Nodding to Ed, he stepped
down, left the gelding at the rack behind the coach, and
moved up the walk. The heavy breakfast he had eaten
less than two hours ago turned to stone as a woman
stepped through the hotel doorway, shading her eyes
against the morning's bright stab of sun.

Wherever she went, Ellen Dunbridge Sinclair instantly commanded the attention of men. Tall, and with
a sure poise that bespoke complete self-control at all
times, she was strikingly feminine. Dressed now in the
heavy dark skirt, full jacket and high-necked blouse she
had worn for the trip, her full rise of breast, small waist
and mature curve of hip were in no way subdued. Beneath the flaring brim of her hat, which was bound by a
silken scarf tied at her throat, raven black hair lay in
stark contrast to the pale white smoothness of her com-
plexion. Her eyes, shadowed with the fatigue of the
journey, brightened perceptibly as Will moved forward,
taking the hands she extended.

"Will. Oh, Will, darling!" The words, barely whispered,
were a breath bridging the gap of three interminable

years. For a moment she stood against him, cheek pressed
to his shoulder, hands laid flat against his chest, and
though he fought against the memory, these same words
echoed across the vast span of time and space. She had
said on that long dead night, the last time he had seen
her: "I'll come to you, Will. Whenever you're ready.
Whenever you want me to come." She had kissed him
that night, tenderly, and for the greater part of three
years he had held the memory of that kiss and its
promise. Now she had come. But not to him.

She drew back, smiling. Roman followed her into the
hotel's deserted lobby. As casually as possible he in-
quired after Amantha Fowler. She answered him coolly
enough, but her upraised eyes held an intimacy he dared
not admit.

"She's upstairs with Dad," Ellen said. "It seems he had
a fall last night, on some wild goose chase or other." She
added quickly, "Oh, it's nothing serious. He sprained his
hip, I believe the doctor said. Please, Will." She laid a
hand on his arm as he glanced at the stairs. "We've only
now just arrived. And—we may have so little time alone,
you and I."

Will Roman drew in a breath, then let it drain out as
if it could empty his being of all that she had meant to
him through long, dead years.

"Yes," he said dully. "I got your letter, Ellen. And I
understood—as I understand now." He sought for words,
and finally found them. "I wish you and Reno all the
best, lass. And, well, I want you to know there will never
be any need for you to reproach yourself where I'm
concerned."

It was a clumsy and awkward speech, he knew, but he
was not prepared for her little gasp of disbelief, or the
stirring of anger in her eyes.

"Reproach myself?" She raised her hand to her mouth,
and as fast as it had come, her anger died. Her eyes
sparkled and for a moment he thought she would laugh.
She came to him then, pressing her cheek against his
neck and holding him tightly.

"Oh, Will, Will! What have I done to you? Have I
really hurt you so much?"

Yet he was certain that he detected an inner amusement at play beneath her surface concern. The thought that she might be teasing him rankled, but he forced himself to smile. On impulse he took her face in his hands and kissed her lightly on the mouth. Her lips were startled beneath his own, and before she could react he broke the kiss. "I think I'll live, lass. Right now I'd better look in on Ben."

He took a long stride toward the staircase before he saw the girl who had paused several steps below the landing.

"I—I'm sorry, Will. I didn't mean to—"

"It's all right, Laurie," Will said, and she came hesitantly down the steps. Laurie Carstairs was still blushing at having intruded at such a moment, but she behaved quite calmly as Will made the introductions. The swift, calculating appraisal in Ellen's eyes drew Roman's attention involuntarily to a comparison between the two.

All resemblance between Laurie Carstairs and Ellen Sinclair ended with their equality in height. Ellen had been reared on the Texas Box, but there remained in her now no hint of the tomboyish hellion she once had been. Laurie's worn Levis, heel-run boots and faded shirt were in striking contrast to Ellen's feminine dress, yet the difference between them went far deeper than mere clothing. Perhaps it was the security, the relative luxury in which Ellen had grown to womanhood which gave her the greater poise and self-assurance. Yet even as Ellen, barely nodding in acknowledgment of the introduction, swept past the girl toward the stairs, Roman felt the rise of a solid compassion toward the younger woman. Pausing at the foot of the stairs, Ellen turned, gazing fixedly at Laurie.

"Carstairs—" She frowned lightly, pondering the name. "Wasn't that the name of the thief and murderer Reno and Dad were chasing last night?" Her expression brightened apologetically. "But of course there could be no connection, I'm sure. You might come up, Will, as soon as you're free. I'm sure Dad has a few things he would like to talk over with you."

Riding south out of Judith City an hour later, Will
Roman left the main road that continued on over the
Gap, swinging up toward the hills in a westerly direction
along the meandering course of Dog Creek. Though the
air was clear and cold, the direct rays of the midmorning
sun warmed his back. As he mounted the first sloping
rise of the Judith range, his irritation gradually gave way
to a measure of calm.

Actually he did not blame Ben Fowler for being per-
turbed over the Carstairs affair. But, suffering from a
dislocated hip, the result of a fall from his horse last
night, the old man had stated his displeasure in out-
rageous terms. Roman had not been prepared for the
angry words of accusation, uttered before Reno, Ellen
and Amantha Fowler, concerning Will's differences with
Engstrand as well as his handling of Carstairs' capture.
Already stung by Ellen's treatment of Laurie Carstairs
only a few minutes earlier, Will had taken his tongue-
lashing with red ears and bowed head. Later, upon com-
ing·downstairs, Roman had not been surprised to see Sam
Engstrand, accompanied by Jere and young Mark, step
down from their horses before the hotel. Realizing that
nothing could be accomplished by meeting Engstrand at
this time, Will had stepped into Ed's bar as the two elder
Engstrands crossed the lobby and mounted the stairs.

Now, as he topped the rise of a long, footing ridge
above the creek and reined on into the timber of the
higher hills, he strove to put all thought of the past hour
from mind. Reno, aided by half of Will's own crew as
well as the six Box riders he had brought north from
Texas, was to begin work at once on his new Slash D
headquarters. Also, Reno had insisted upon making a
cut of Ellen's stock from the various herds, regardless of
the lateness of season. Roman had objected to nothing
and made his excuses as quickly as possible—before Ben
again broached the subject of Dusty's re-employment.

Since leaving the valley he had ridden with no particular sense of urgency. The chore he had set himself now,
he knew, should have been attended to immediately after
Jack Carstairs' escape—and would have been, if his differences with Sam Engstrand had not obscured his judg-

ment at the time. He crested the final rise at the lower
end of Dog Creek Meadow and glanced back. He saw a
single rider coming up through the scattered timber
below. A certain familiarity about horse and rider held
him there, and a few minutes later he recognized Dusty
Wilson's spare, wiry form. The little tophand was grinning as he drew up beside Will at the foot of the meadow.

"Figured you might need some company on this little
visit you're plannin' to make," he drawled casually. "Me,
I'm not much on herdin' a buggy. I drove into town.
Figured Reno could take it from there."

Will rolled a smoke, struck a match and held it out
for Dusty. "Pretty sure where I was headed, weren't
you, son?"

Dusty shrugged. "Man makes a mistake, it don't follow
he has to leave it that way. Course, we'd had a lot better
chance of cinchin' the deal if we'd headed up this way
last night. But, what the hell, a man can't pick 'em every
time."

Striking directly across the meadow, Roman noticed
several groupings of the Kesslers' KK stock. Several of
these lower meadows, such as this one on Dog Creek,
would provide good winter graze for the cattle Frank
and Dobe ran higher up during the summer months. And
also, Will thought as he mapped the surrounding country
in his mind's eye, these dozens of small mountain
meadows which cluttered the timbered benchlands for
miles upon end, would serve ideally as secret holding
pens and waystations for any rustled stock driven up
from the valley below. Almost any of these meadows
could accommodate several hundred head temporarily.
And by easy stages such stock could be driven south and
east toward the Judith Gap.

None of the stock here, however, bore any marking
except the Kesslers' KK brand. Nor had Roman expected
anything else. As he struck the trail above the meadow,
climbing through the timber ahead of Dusty's mount,
he knew that neither the Kesslers nor any happenchance
band of rustlers would allow stolen stock to remain long
in these lower meadows.

Both Will and Dusty had ranged much of the bench-

land country to the west of the basin the first year they
had come north, but since that time they had been too
busy to investigate these slopes. Too, the Kesslers, pushing up through the Gap the next year had pre-empted
this portion of the Judiths as their accustomed range.
During the prior winter, though Roman had known them
to be having a hard time of it, Frank and Dobe Kessler
had neither asked for help nor accepted it when offered.
They kept well to themselves, and as far as anyone knew
there had been no evidence connecting them with the
increasing losses of stock along the Judith.

Nevertheless, Will had not been able to bring himself
to trust the two men. Possibly some unknown band of
outlaws was operating upon the valley herds, but Roman
did not see how they could do so without the Kesslers'
knowledge. In Jack Carstairs, Will had held a key. For
this reason—as well as for Laurie's sake—he had brought
Jack in. Yet Jack had escaped. The only answer—the
only possible answer—lay somewhere in these hills.

It was nearly noon when Roman swung off the trail
and followed a ridge which would bring him out well
above the Kessler place. The spruce and fir gave way to
tall, straight pine and an occasional clump of aspen.
Fnally, drawing up on a protruding knoll, Will gestured
toward the log house and outbuildings of the Kesslers'
headquarters several hundred feet below. At this height
he and Dusty could see over the intervening ridges to
the valley, blue-wrapped in haze beyond. Circling around
to their right, a ridge dropped away from their present
position, its timber-clad bulk forming the south wall en-
closing the meadow of the KK ranch.

Scanning the run of this hogbacked ridge, Roman
caught the pencil-thin rise of what appeared to be a
streamer of smoke fading into the air from its opposite
side. From this elevation he could see but a small semi-
circle of the meadow which lay over the ridge.

"I wouldn't be surprised, boy." Dusty's voice startled
him slightly. "I wouldn't be surprised but what we've
run our little bird into the ground."

Thirty minutes later, as they dropped down through
the timber along the southern slope of the ridge, Roman

reined in to inspect a small cabin directly below. Though
it faced a small meadow, the cabin was set well back
against the slope and might easily have gone unnoticed
but for the thin tendril of smoke from its chimney.
Against one cabin wall a lean-to projected outward,
roofed over and walled at the back. As he moved cautiously downgrade, Roman saw the hindquarters of two
horses beneath the shelter. He was within ten yards of
the cabin when a movement off to his right caught his
attention.

The man, carrying a bucket which he evidently had
filled from the creek nearby, was a complete stranger to
Will. He had approached to within twenty feet of the
two mounted men when one of the sheltered horses
whinnied suddenly and he glanced up, startled. Roman's
gun came smoothly to hand as the man cursed, dropping
the bucket and clawing for his low-slung weapon. Will's
shot blasted flatly in the thin air. The roughly dressed
stranger froze into position as Will's bullet *thunked* into
the soft earth at his feet. Will eased his mount into the
clearing, then halted as a familiar voice broke from the
cabin off to his left.

"All right, Roman. That's far enough. One squeeze of
my finger and you're through right there!"

The man in front of Will raised a hand, pointing off
up the slope.

"There's another'n here, Dobe! Better watch your step!"

Will did not move. Dobe Kessler spoke again.

"Call him down, Roman. Now! I couldn't noways miss
from here and it wouldn't take much to talk me into
droppin' you where you sit."

Will saw no sign of Dusty, but called his name. The
little tophand eased into the open on the cabin's far side.
For an instant Dobe Kessler, standing half revealed in
the cabin's doorway, seemed to waver between the two
mounted men.

"Sorry, Dobe." Casually Roman reholstered his weapon.
"Your friend here was a little quick about reaching for
his gun. I didn't have time to argue."

Stepping outside, the younger Kessler held his carbine
at the ready. With his long muscular arms, heavy shoul-

ders and short sloping brow, he reminded Will of a gorilla. Anger sparked plainly in Dobe's one good eye.

"Damn it, you're lucky I didn't drill you where you stand," Dobe said. "You're off your range, hombre. You got any business with Frank or me, it's a good idea to come up the front way, understand?"

Roman rolled himself a smoke. "Sure, Dobe. I understand." He eyed the man narrowly above the flare of the match. "Dusty and me, we figured we might get a line on young Carstairs up this way. Ain't happened to see him about?"

"Carstairs? What the hell would a two-bit rustler like Carstairs be doin' up here?" Dobe's scowl deepened, his one blind eye leering sightlessly into space. "You ain't sayin' we had anything to do with that—" Suddenly he cut off in mid-sentence, a slow rise of color showing upon the harsh, weathered planes of his face. Roman exhaled smoke leisurely.

"That what, Dobe? You mean that little jailbreak last night?" He shifted easily in the saddle, right hand within inches of his gun. "If I recall it correctly, Dobe, you and your brother rode out of town fairly early last night. Before we brought Jack in, matter of fact. News seems to travel pretty fast in these hills."

"So what if it does?" Dobe said.

Will flipped his cigarette into the meadow grass.

"Dobe," he said quietly, "if it's all right with you, I'd like to take a little look inside that cabin."

Dobe Kessler's eye swung once toward Wilson and back to Will. He said, "Bert, Roman and his segundo are ridin' out now. Remember what these two gents look like. Next time you see either one of 'em back here on the bench you'll know what to do."

For a long silent minute Will did not move. He flicked a glance at the half opened door and the shadows inside the small cabin. He looked at the two horses in the lean-to shelter. Only one wore its saddle, but that fact alone proved nothing. And there was no denying that he and Dusty were intruders on KK range. He nodded finally, the faintest ghost of a smile touching his mouth.

"Looks like you boys have been taking on some new hands. Business been picking up, Dobe?"

"Yeah. And we're liable to take on some more, seein' the trouble we're havin' with trespassers these days." Dobe gestured with the rifle. "That's the way out. And there's no use stoppin' by the house. Frank ain't got no more to say than I have, savvy?"

As Will Roman and Dusty Wilson reined off across the meadow toward the lower end of the hogbacked ridge, Dobe Kessler swore softly, feeling tension drain from his body. The man called Bert, whom he and Frank had hired along with three others last week, looked after the two men. Bert was a rangy, ill-kempt fellow who wore his gun-holster low and tight against his thigh, secured by a rawhide thong.

"That's him, eh?" Bert said with easy contempt. "Hell, we could have spoiled 'em both between us and the thing 'would have been done. What you waitin' on?"

Dobe glared at the man. "What the hell was you waitin' on? I noticed you didn't get far with your try!"

"He was holdin' aces before I could draw. It won't happen again."

Dobe turned toward the door. "It'd better not," he said. "It better not happen on KK grass, either. Frank gave you boys the word. When Roman goes it's got to look like the Engstrand bunch pulled the job. Frank and me, we've got a good spot here and we figure to stay in business, understand?"

As Dobe raised a hand to push the door open he found Jack Carstairs standing close against the opening. The anger that was already in him flared, and with the same hand he pushed the younger man flat in the face, sending him sprawling along the wall and into the tiered bunk-ends beyond. Carstairs' head cracked solidly against the end of the upper bunk. Holding the back of his head with both hands, he staggered forward, trying to maintain his balance.

"Dammit, Dobe," he wailed. "I wasn't doin' nothing. Ain't no call to—"

"I told you to keep away from that door! A nice mess we'd had on our hands if Roman spotted you skulking

around in here. And you wanted us to let you keep
your cayuse up here!" Dobe snorted. "You think those
two rannahans would be ridin' off nice and peaceful-
like right now if they'd spotted an extra horse out there?"

A rill of soft, but contemptuous laughter turned Dobe.
In the open doorway, the gunman Bert jerked his head at
Carstairs.

"Why don't we get rid o' the punk?" Bert said. "Playin'
nursemaid's damned poor work for a man."

"When you get tired of it, hombre, just say so! There's
others would like your pay!"

Dobe moved to a table that was littered with dirty tin
plates and utensils, lifted a bottle and took a drink from
its neck. The liquor warmed his stomach and he grinned
at Carstairs who was sitting upon the lower bunk, head
in hands.

"No, Bert," he said, "we're not getting rid of the punk.
Whether you know it or not, Jack here is just about the
biggest drawin' card we got in our business now. Yes
sir, Mister Jack Carstairs is goin' to be with us for some
time to come."

CHAPTER V

Ellen Sinclair was depressed by the crude ugliness of the ranch house at Box. As she rode up the gentle slope with Amantha Fowler and Reno beside her, and with Ben complaining from the buggy's back seat at each jolting rut that jarred his injured hip, the squat log-walled structure appeared vastly more primitive and uninviting than she had expected. Here was no vast and roomy building with tall windows and wide verandas such as Ben Fowler owned in Texas and in which she had grown to womanhood. The headquarters of the Montana Box was severely square, the rough-hewn chinked logs of its outer façade relieved only by a small front porch reaching less than halfway across the building's width. Nor were the rooms inside any better. Unlined walls and bare, whipsawn plank floors, splintery underfoot. The crudest of battered furniture. Ellen barely nodding at China John, whom she had not seen in three years. She retired at once to the room she and Reno were to share, leaving the others to help the injured rancher inside.

She stared with distaste at the chipped enamel bedstead, the dim and wavering glass above the scarred dresser. There were no chairs, nor was there any sign of a closet for the trunks full of clothes which were coming on with the furniture for the house Reno had yet to build. The single unshaded and uncurtained window admitted barely enough light to dispell the gloom. It was warm, and as she removed her hat and jacket, tossing them upon the bed, she heard the shuffling footsteps of her husband and Ben moving slowly past the door to the adjoining room.

Had the whole thing been a mistake—perhaps the greatest mistake she was ever to make in life? Even now Ellen could not clearly isolate the emotion which had ruled her when she met Will Roman in town. Once more. she felt a fleeting anger at the words he had used. Hold herself responsible indeed! With an annoyed flounce she went to the window, fluffing her hair with the fingers of both hands.

Footsteps came down the short hall. Ellen's frown deepened momentarily as Reno entered the room without knocking. She winced at the squeaking protest of the springs as he sat on the bed. Unbidden, the errant thought entered her mind that Will would have respected her desire for privacy, as he would have—and indeed once had—divined many of her small and unspoken desires. Yet she had married Reno. Reno. . . .

Ellen Sinclair swung around, studying the man she had married. His back was turned toward her, his light blond hair curling upon his neck, and for an instant this too seemed to add to her irritation. Married hardly a month, he could at least pay some attention to his wife's comfort in these first minutes of settling into their temporary home!

She said crossly, "I hope you had your fun last night —not that it makes any difference that Dad might be laid up for several weeks."

He turned without getting up from the bed. He was frowning, as if he had been thinking of something else and was aware of her presence only because she had spoken. Ellen was sure he smiled only with effort.

"Chasing around the country with a posse's not my idea of fun, old girl." He glanced idly about the room. "Not much of a place at that, is it?"

Eyeing his profile—the bold sweep of brow, straight nose, heavy lips and firm chin—Ellen felt a sudden warmth come over her. He was a handsome brute, Reno, and perhaps his mood of preoccupation had been for her sake after all. She rounded the bed, coming to stand before him.

"It will do," she said softly. "And it's not as though it

were really our home. I'm sure you'll build us a much
nicer place, darling."

She had placed a hand on his shoulder, running her
fingers up the line of his neck in a gentle caress. His sudden grimace took her by surprise. She stepped back as
Reno lurched to his feet, striding about the small room to
stare sightlessly out the window.

"I'll build us a headquarters. second to none," he
ground out abruptly. "We'll have the biggest and fanciest
house this side of Denver. Damn it, I aim to make Slash
the richest spread in Montana and if anybody gets in
my way—"

"But, darling—" Puzzled, yet pleasantly so, she came
up behind him. "Who would want to get in your way?
We have no enemies here. What makes you—"

"Don't be too sure of that," Reno cut in ominously.
"Roman's already got Box in bad with the Engstrands
and Kesslers. They're the biggest outfits in the basin
outside of Box and Slash. That's why I told Ben I was
insisting on a cut right away. We've got to break free of
Box. Of Roman's damned meddling. Yes, and of the old
man's influence, too. I'm on my own now and that's the
way I'm going to stay!"

His vehemence startled Ellen. She said, "You mean we,
don't you, darling? We're on our own."

"We. I. What the hell? It's all the same, ain't it?" He
turned, staring at her. "Meeting Roman hasn't made any
difference, has it? You haven't gone soft on Will again?"

Ellen stomped her foot, vexed yet unable to control
the burning of her cheeks at this obvious insinuation.
Reno said nastily, "Well, well. So the old flame burns
again, eh? Or did it ever go out?"

Ellen felt her anger solidify into a calm, deadly fury.
She whispered, "I married you, Reno—a fact which you
seem to remember well enough in terms of Slash D
stock."

"Hey! Whoa, there, old girl!" His laughter burst free.
He took her by the shoulders. Without warning he bent
and kissed her upon the mouth. She jerked away. He
reached for her again and as she sought to avoid his

grasp she felt the bed at the backs of her knees. She fell and Reno's weight came heavily down upon her.

There was no laughter in his eyes now as he bent above her upon the bed, searching for her mouth with his own. She continued to avoid him, straining her head to one side upon the spread. He shifted one hand, grasped her tightly by the hair, and forced the kiss.

It was a silent, struggling embrace. She could feel teeth against her bruised mouth, the rasp of whiskers against her chin. Yet suddenly, and without the slightest lag of intensity, fury blended into passion, touching flame to body and mind. His hands were upon her and conscious thought ceased to exist. There was no knowing, or not knowing, no passage of time. The world caught fire, all existence a mounting pulsation that was beyond reality, its end as violent, as shatteringly final as death itself.

He left her alone. Long, long minutes passed before she stirred to a full awareness of her disarranged condition. She lay for a further time, frowning as she became slowly conscious of the direction of her thoughts. Weirdly, she was not think about Reno, but about Will Roman. Why had the sight of that rustler's woman—*what was her name? Carstairs? Laurie Carstairs?*—so infuriated her this morning in town? Could Will, *her* Will—really be involved with such a common, washed-out wench?

But no. This was impossible. Will Roman had known nothing of her marriage to Reno Sinclair until he received her letter a month ago. For Will, any sort of affection came only with time, and faithlessness was certainly not one of his faults. As she got to her feet, carefully straightening her clothes, Ellen Dunbridge Sinclair assured herself that Mrs. Laurie Carstairs could not possibly evoke anything more than a passing sympathy in Will Roman. Will, whether he knew it or not, was still hers, hers to command, and he would remain so. Ellen had no realization of her own selfishness and impropriety where Will was concerned. She had only a sure knowledge of her power over men.

Someone knocked on her door. She heard Amantha's inquiring voice. With a final glimpse in the wavering mirror over the dresser, she straightened her hair, then crossed the room. She did not think of Reno as she opened the door. She stepped into the hallway, smiling at the little gray-haired woman who had mothered her since childhood, and the mantle of depression which had been upon her seemed to disappear.

It was well into the afternoon when Will and Dusty left the Kessler place. Swinging aside from the trail less than a mile below the ranch, Will led out on a course along the northering slopes to the west of the valley. For over an hour neither man spoke, though both continually studied the timbered slopes and occasional meadows through which they passed. They had dropped down from the greater heights through a series of four staggered meadows along the same creek when Will drew up on the barren summit of a ridge. Below, and to the east, several steep-walled ravines and lesser spurs gave way toward the valley floor, turning slowly darker with shadow.

"Well, boss, I'd say we pulled a blank all around on this little deal." Dusty spat dryly as he reined in beside Will. "In my book it's treys to deuces Dobe and Frank's guilty as seven kinds of hell on the Carstairs deal. But what we got for a call?"

There being no ready answer, Will Roman reached for tobacco and paper. The day's ride had produced little or no information. Beyond the fact that Frank and Dobe Kessler had hired on at least four new hands recently— which might or might not be indicative of illegal intent —he had learned nothing further about the jailbreak in town, or about any possible alliances Jack Carstairs might have made in his raiding of the basin herds. Nowhere along the benchlands had he and Dusty seen a single head of stock wearing any but the KK brand, and at the main ranch, Frank's welcome had been hardly less defiant than Dobe's.

Glancing at Wilson, Roman once more pondered Ben Fowler's intentions toward the little tophand. Several times today he had attempted to mention the matter to Dusty, yet could not rid himself of the thought that Ben might be persuaded to change his mind. Actually, Dusty might quit Box rather than follow such orders. Nor would Reno's objections be less violent. Damn it, Ben Fowler was attempting to treat grown men like children. No man likes to feel that his life is being directed by the hand of another, and Will felt a strong resentment against Ben for involving him in such a course. At this moment, however, he was saved the necessity of words by Dusty's grunt as he concentrated on some distant object.

"Looks like some ranny's cookin' up a real bonfire," Dusty commented. "Looks like it might be over at the Flushings', or maybe the Carstairs place."

Following the direction of Dusty's finger, Roman saw the mushrooming rise of a gray-black column of smoke beyond a lesser ridge to the north and east. Though the last of the sun's light had been eclipsed by the towering mountains behind them, the mounting pillar of smoke rediscovered its setting rays as it climbed quickly over the broken land.

Rapidly calculating his own position, Will came to a sure conclusion: that column was rising directly over the Carstairs place. At the same moment he recalled Sam Engstrand's promise that Jack Carstairs would hang. He said, "Dusty, let's go," and put his mount down the slope of the dwindling ridge.

Upon the lower, broken slopes the heavier stand of pine gave way to occasional clumps of cottonwood, with alder and willow in the creek-lined bottoms and blue-green sage that clawed at their horses' legs. Thirty minutes later, as they topped a barren rise well down toward the basin floor, Roman reined in hard. Squinting, he made out the figures of three mounted men heading south along the foot of the hills. Dusty braked his lathered mount to a halt beside Will.

"Figures like it to me." The little puncher echoed Roman's own thoughts as he traced the course of the trio from the area where they had last seen the rising smoke. The riders below were all but indistinguishable in the growing dusk. Will spurred downgrade.

Setting his course at a slant that would intercept the three men near the mouth of a shallow ravine, Will saw them break into a run. He was urging the roan to an even greater effort when a hollow appeared before him, breaking the animal's stride. The gelding, attempting to recover, struck the opposite rise off balance and went down in a forward, rolling spill that threw Roman clear of the saddle. He landed with a bone-crushing impact and though he rolled with his forward movement he took several minutes in getting to his feet.

He had lost his forty-five and spent a good five minutes more finding it in the rapidly fading light. The roan, apparently not much the worse for wear, stood idly nearby. Will had regained the saddle when Dusty rode back through the dusk.

"Spooked," Dusty said. "Spooked plenty, whoever they are. But from where we stand and the way they're headed, I'd say there was just about one place they could go."

"Yeah," Roman said. "Kesslers'." But he had to determine what had happened at the Carstairs place as well as establish the identity of those three men. He said, "Follow them, Dusty. Find out where they're going and who they are. We'll meet later in town."

Dusty started off, then came back.

"What if I catch me a handful of Engstrands on this little deal?" he asked quietly. "Wouldn't surprise me none but what Sam's about riled enough to pull this stunt. And it could be he's figuring to swing Frank and Dobe in line."

Roman recalled Ruby Ferguson's warning about this very thing. Yet, knowing Sam Engstrand, Will shook his head.

"If it's Sam and his boys, it could be he's figuring to shake Frank down to get his hands on Jack. Keep your eye open, Dusty, but stay out of it if things get hot."

"You're the boss," Dusty said. "But I say you're givin' Sam too damned much credit for riding the straight and narrow. After that beatin' you gave him he wouldn't care how a man smelled, long as he's willin' to face up to Box."

Will did not argue the point. He rode off through the darkness toward the cabin Jack Carstairs had built on

Alder Creek. It took him twenty minutes of steady travel along the edge of hills to reach the stream and another ten to crest the low rise beyond which lay the tiny valley Carstairs had staked out as his own two years ago.

For some time he had seen the glow of the fire, but the flames had burned well down when he rode into the hollow. All that remained of the house and barn were two square beds of hotly glowing coals that cast a dull radiance over the yard, brightening now and again as a tongue leaped hopefully skyward, only to be submerged once more.

The heat reached out across the flat, pressing not unpleasantly against Roman's face and chest as he brought the nervous gelding to a stand. His own nerves tightened as a horse nickered from the darkness beyond the glowing rubble. He drew his gun and circled cautiously that way. He was searching the dim outlines of a stand of cottonwood near the creek when someone said:

"Roman? Over here."

Recognizing the dry tones of Amos Flushing, the Carstairs' nearest neighbor, Will skirted a small corral. At its far end he saw two figures standing before their horses. He greeted Flushing and stepped down heavily. Then, in the light of a momentary flareup from the glowing remains of the house, he spied Laurie Carstairs. He moved toward her, seeing the firm, uplifted line of her chin, the play of light and shadow on her chiseled features.

"Jimmy?" As he spoke the name he realized for the first time the true depth of his own anxiety—anxiety that was but partially relieved at finding Laurie herself safe and apparently unharmed. If anything had happened to the boy. . . .

"The little fellow's all right," Flushing said grimly. He was a man of average height, in his middle forties, who had come north with the second drive out of Texas two years ago. "Mrs. Carstairs and the boy were at our place when we saw the fire. We left him with Mrs. Flushing when we rode over."

Laurie Carstairs was staring toward the burning remains of the buildings. Will saw the prone figure of a man on the packed earth close beside the glowing coals of the house. In spite of himself, his first emotion was one of exultation, though he quickly buried this involuntary reaction beneath a feeling of genuine concern as Laurie turned her head, meeting his eyes.

"Reckon he didn't have time, or wasn't lookin' for a fight," Flushing said slowly. "Way it must have happened, I'd say he must have knew the gents and didn't figure on shootin' talk. There was only two shots. We heard 'em plain, coming over the ridge." He paused, adding, "From what I could see, both of 'em took him square in the back."

Will mumured, "Laurie, I don't know what to say. I—"

His voice trailed off beneath her puzzled stare. Her expression cleared suddenly and she stepped forward, laying a hand on his arm.

"It's not Jack," she told him. "It's the man you sent over this morning. It's Hank Crawford, Will."

Roman stood rooted into his tracks. Hank Crawford! How could he have forgotten Hank's presence here at the Carstairs place? Only now was he aware to what extent his preoccupation for Laurie's safety and that of her child must have claimed his mind. He half turned from the girl, unaware of the gathering thunder on his own features, but she held him, her cheek pressed closely against his chest.

"Oh, Will, I'm so sorry. He was an old friend, wasn't he?"

Will nodded, marveling that she had made no mention of her own loss of a home and perhaps livelihood as well. Amos Flushing said gruffly, "Anything I can do, you know I'm ready."

Hardness lay like the clutch of steel in the pit of Will's belly. He had a brief picture of Hank Crawford whittling out a toy sixgun for the boy Will Roman once had been upon the Texas Box.

He said, "Box will take care of it's own," and made a small movement, as though to withdraw from the girl.

Laurie's head came up. And now she was angry. Her whole body seemed to tremble.

"Yes, Box will take care of its own," she said. "But how? Answer me that, Will Roman. By killing and more killing and killing again?" Her voice rose sharply into the first notes of an actual hysteria. "Kill, kill, kill—that's all you know, any of you! Kill them all like you've killed Jack! He's as good as dead, isn't he? Go ahead, Mister Roman! Kill until you can bathe yourself in blood, if that's what you want! Slash and claw and kill until you're killed yourself for all I care!"

He took her into his arms then, and felt her go soft against him. She did not cry, but just stood there, catching at the throbbing gusts of breath that went through her more bitterly than any tears. Minutes passed before she could bring herself to speak.

"How can I bear to bring him up in this kind of world?" she whispered against his chest. And then, lifting her head, "For that matter, how can I bring him up at all, with no home, no father, no—"

He saw that she was on the verge of hysterical laughter and he turned her suddenly, walking her toward her mount. Taking her shoulders into his hands he studied the sweetly rounded lines of her face. Then he bent and kissed her gently upon the mouth; kissed her as he might have kissed a child, lost and lonely and homeless in the night.

"There's nothing wrong with you a little hard work won't fix," he said. "And Ruby Ferguson's had that waiting for you in town a long time now."

CHAPTER VI

It was still short of nine o'clock when Will Roman rode into the yard at Box. Light spilled from the windows of the house. From the open bunkhouse door came the sound of talk and laughter. Two men stepped into the shadows, crossing toward Roman as he reined up before the porch. Reno Sinclair, the foremost of these, frowned at sight of the humped shape which was lashed to the saddle of the led horse. He did not speak. He moved quickly toward the animal, looked at the body, and cursed hollowly.

Roman dismounted. The puncher who had come up. with Reno called across the yard to the bunkhouse:

"It's Hank. Hank Crawford. Somebody's done him in!"

Men stirred into the yard as Roman, ignoring Reno and the others alike, climbed the steps of the porch. The door opened before he had touched the knob. Ellen's smile melted into blank bewilderment as Roman brushed past her.

"Why, Will, what on earth—"

He gave her no attention, but crossed the room and went down the short hallway to the back bedroom. Ben Fowler, eyes closed, was sitting propped up in the bed while his wife read to him from a book she held close to the lamplight. The tiny gray-haired woman glanced up at Roman's entrance. Ben turned his head on the pillows, frowning as he opened his eyes.

Will told Ben what had happened at the Carstairs place. He did not realize the finality of his own intentions until the old man spoke.

"So now you figure to throw every available man into

62

the saddle and go on the warpath—eh, boy?" Ben grimaced as he pushed himself further upright in the bed. His gaze sharpened intently on Will.

"I don't know how this whole thing started, son," he said, "but it looks to me like you're building a personal grudge into something that might get out of hand."

Roman felt his face grow warm. He was aware that both Ellen and Reno had come to the door and were, for the second time this day, witness to his censure at old Ben's hand.

"Ben," he said distinctly, "Hank Crawford was shot in the back. He was your friend as well as mine. How personal does a thing have to get before a man has a right to get sore?"

"That's not the point, boy. Whoever killed Hank will hang for it. But that's not to say a man has to go on the warpath against his neighbors every time some shenanigan is pulled. No matter what kind of personal differences you might have with Sam Engstrand, we'll get the straight of the thing before we start fillin' the air with lead."

The old man's tone left no room for argument. Well, damn it, he'd just have to make room.

Will said, "I've spent three years building up the Judith, Ben. You aiming to take over now?" And then he realized that he had struck more deeply than he intended. Muscles tightened the faintly sagging line of Fowler's jaw. His gnarled hand knotted tightly upon the bedspread.

"Will, you've been like a son to me for over twenty years. I'd hate to see you get too big for your pants at a time like this."

Though an inner voice demanded caution, Roman said, "Dusty's riding trail on the three who killed Hank and burned the Carstairs place. I warned him against making a play on his own. But when I meet him in town tonight something's liable to give."

He started to turn away. The old man called him back.

"Just a minute, Will!" The old rancher made a visible, though unsuccessful effort to relax. "Fact of the matter is, I'm sending Reno out with the word that every

rancher in the basin is to show up here at Box tomorrow
night. We'll get this thing thrashed out the way it should
be—amongst us all. And without killing each other off,
if we can help it."

As Fowler's glance shifted to Reno, Will understood
that he was making an effort to avoid an open breach
between them. To Sinclair, Ben said, "I figured· on
sending you out in the morning, but maybe it's best you
make the rounds tonight. This way you can check on
who's home and who's not. And tell them I want every
mother's son here on Box at eight tomorrow night.
Understand?"

Roman walked past Reno and Ellen and stepped into
the hall. Ben Fowler called after him:

"If you're ridin' in to meet Wilson tonight you'll do
it alone, boy! No rider of mine's stirrin' a stump off Box
till after the meetin' tomorrow night!"

Moving down the hall to the enormous kitchen at
the rear of the house, Roman heard Reno's complaining
voice, followed by several explosive and conclusive re-
marks from Ben. China John, silent and grinning, poured
coffee into a cup at the table as Will sat down heavily
at one end. John busied himself at the stove, and when
Will heard Reno stomp out of the house several minutes
later he was well into his meal. He was on his third
cup of coffee when Ellen came into the room.

"Will—" She seemed hesitant as she sat lightly upon
one end of the bench running the length of the oilcloth-
covered table. "Do you really think you're right about
Sam Engstrand? Right enough, I mean, to go against
Dad this way?"

She was wearing a pale blue dress which accented the
blueness of her eyes, heightening their contrast against
the raven black mass of her hair. It was this contrast
of eyes and hair which had remained so vividly in his
dreams of Ellen during these past three years: a contrast at once striking, and appealingly feminine. That
Ellen Sinclair had lost neither appeal nor femininity
was self-evident, yet Will could not help but recall the
incident of this same morning when Ellen had dismissed
Laurie Carstairs with a contempt that bespoke sheer

cruelty. It had been unlike her—unlike the Ellen Dunbridge he had known nearly all his life—and for a moment Will wondered how much she had changed in other ways. He shrugged, took a final bite of steak from his plate and chewed it thoroughly. Ellen frowned.

"It couldn't be that he's right, could it?" she said. "From the way you talked to that—that rustler's woman this morning, I—"

"You what, Ellen?" he asked mildly. "You think I'm after Sam's hide because of what he said about Laurie Carstairs? Where did you hear it, by the way?"

She flushed.

"What does it matter?" she demanded. "The fact that I did hear it—that everyone's talking about you and that —that—" She bit her lip, glancing warily across the room at the cook. China John shuffled out the back door and she returned to the attack.

"How could you do it, Will? I don't see—a woman like that—why, Reno says she even has a child!"

Will rose deliberately from his chair. "Even?" He smiled as he whispered the word, but his eyes were dark. She came up at once, impatient now.

"Will Roman, you know very well what I mean. And I can't say that I admire your taste. You might at least have paid me the respect of—of—"

"Of waiting until you got here so you could pass judgment for me? Or did you just want me to hang around until you got tired of Reno?"

She gasped at the taunt, then controlled the fury that followed.

"If you won't think of me," she said coldly, "you might at least think of Dad—and of Box. Whether you know it or not, he went to a lot of trouble this morning to calm Sam Engstrand down. If you must have your brawls over these common women you might pick a man nearer your own age and with the understanding you are not using Box to back your spite."

Will's face was pale. The line of his mouth had grown tight as she spoke, but now it relaxed with an odd, resigned finality.

"For your information, Mrs. Sinclair," he said, "a man

was murdered tonight. I think Sam Engstrand or one of his boys did the job. When I find out for sure, I'll know what to do. As for my getting into brawls over common women—" He shook his head, and then he grinned. "Don't you think you've strained your credit a little, Ellen?"

He was at the door when she called his name. Turning, he met her rush as she threw herself against him. She clung to him tightly. She sobbed broken, unfinished phrases against his chest. He held her off at arm's length.

"You've made your choice, lass," he said gently. "Don't you think we'd better leave it that way?"

Ten minutes later, freshly mounted, he rode toward town.

For a man who recently had married comparative wealth and security, as well as the woman of his choice, Reno Sinclair was far from happy. Leaving the Boxed F headquarters well ahead of Will Roman, Reno spurred directly south, keeping on at a steady pace until he struck the winding course of Frenchman's Creek. The sky was clear and the moon's pale light plainly outlined the rolling contours of the land. Willow and cottonwood cast dark shadows along the banks of the stream as he crossed it, swinging west toward the Freeman place, a mile farther on.

Light spilled into the yard from an unshaded window as he reined up before the small house. Without dismounting he called the rancher's name. The door opened and the lanky, bent figure of Henry Freeman appeared.

"The old man wants you at Box tomorrow night," Reno said, harshly impatient. "Pass the word on to Flushing and the rest. Eight o'clock sharp."

"Who?" the old man thrust his head forward, as if by this act his eyes could better penetrate the uncertain light. "Oh, Sinclair. Sorry, boy, but I reckon you'll have to make the rounds yourself. The missus ain't feelin' none too well and—"

"Eight o'clock tomorrow night," Reno repeated. "And you'll tell Flushing and the others. Those are orders, understand?"

Without waiting for a reply Reno sank spur to his

mount, tearing out of the yard. His resentment at having been appointed Ben Fowler's messenger boy somewhat dissipated by relegating the duty to Freeman, he
continued on in a southwesterly direction, crossing the
main road and striking the hills well west of the Gap.

Avoiding the trail he had used last night, he grew in-
creasingly alert as he climbed into the timber country
below the bench. Dusty Wilson might pop up at any
time, and despite the outward legitimacy of his errand
he didn't want to meet Dusty. As he picked his way
upgrade through the light and deep shadow of moon
and timber, Reno fretted over the problem of Jack Carstairs' continued existence.

Damn Frank and Dobe Kessler to hell! On top of
everything else, why should they pick a time like this to
burn the Carstairs place and kill—of all people—Hank
Crawford, one of Box's oldest and most reliable hands?
Damnation, you'd think gunning down Slim Olsen would
be enough for a while. At least that had been necessary
in order to break Carstairs free. But this! This beat all.

Reno was certain, however, that Frank Kessler had not
acted without good and sufficient reason. He was a
shrewd one, Kessler, and nobody's fool—as Reno himself
had good cause to know. He was skirting the first of the
small mountain meadows in the silvery moonlight when
the full truth came to him. Involuntarily, he drew up for
a moment, reluctantly admiring the motives which must
lie beneath Kessler's latest act.

Who had Will Roman blamed for Hank Crawford's
death and the burning of the Carstairs place? Sam Engstrand, of course. And who would Frank Kessler expect
Roman to blame? Sam Engstrand, again. Reno grinned,
almost laughed. It was a neat piece of work, one that
might yet bust the valley wide open regardless of old
Ben's attempts to hold the basin ranchers together.

Yet at the same time, as he spurred on up the slope
above the small meadow, Reno realized that his own
position remained unchanged. As long as Jack Carstairs
lived—and was likely holed up somewhere under the
Kesslers' thumbs—Reno Sinclair would have to dance to
the tune they played. A complete break between Fowler's

Box and Engstrand's Chair might make excellent pickings
for the Kesslers. They could remain aloof, playing each
side against the other, while he, Reno. . . .

He drew up abruptly, holding his breath as he listened
more intently for the small sound he thought he had
heard. The trail, dappled occasionally by the moon's
eerie light through the branches overhead, lay half revealed along the sloping ridge he was following. The
sound came again: the muffled but certain tread of hoofs
on soft earth. For the barest fraction of a second, before
his common sense told him how unlikely were his
chances, he had the swift, rising hope that he had stumbled upon Jack Carstairs, alone and perhaps riding down
to round up a few head of basin stock.

Drawing his gun, he reined gently aside from the trail.
He chose a vantage point of deep shadow that overlooked
an open break of moonlight on the trail, and leaned forward, covering his horse's nostrils with a cautioning hand.

His thinning hopes that the oncoming rider might be
Carstairs evaporated as the approaching hoofbeats testi-
fied to the presence of several animals. A few moments
later the first of three mounted men appeared in the open
space less than thirty feet away. As the other two followed, Reno studied their hat-shadowed features, straining to catch some familiar item of posture or gear.

He ground his teeth in sheer suspense, but identified
none of the three. Passing into the shadow farther downtrail, one of the men laughed softly and said, "Hell, I
told you all the time this was the way to play it, Pa.
Roman won't know what hit him before we're through."

Surprise jarred up in Reno as he recognized the voice
of Jere Engstrand and his father's grunting unintelligible
answer. As the three Engstrands—he was sure the third
had been Matt, the second eldest son—dropped on downtrail, Reno found himself held motionless by an unreasoning resentment. Will—of course Will had been
right, as he seemed to be right about so many things.

So it had been Sam and his boys who burned the Carstairs place and killed Hank. And evidently they had
made some kind of deal with Frank and Dobe against
Box. But where, as owner of the new Slash D, would

this leave him? Unaware of the passing of time, Reno
continued to sit his mount in the deep shadow of the
pine. So involved were his speculations that he failed
to hear the approach of another rider until the mounted
figure was outlined almost directly before him on the
moonlit trail.

Jack Carstairs, Reno thought. *Jack Carstairs!*

Recognition and action came as one. Reno's gun slid
from his holster almost unbidden. The searspring made
a dull metallic click as the hammer came back beneath
his thumb. He squeezed the trigger as the rider's head
turned, tilting up with alarm.

The recoil jarred solidly up Reno's wrist and arm,
the blast slamming away through the trees along the
slope. Twenty feet away, the man in the saddle jerked
stiffly upright. His weapon, already clear of its holster
despite the briefness of warning, fired harmlessly into
the earth before he fell.

Spurring forward, Reno grabbed at the reins of the
riderless mount. He circled back and stared down at
the fallen man, feeling oddly apprehensive. He stepped
down with stiff legs, knelt and rolled the man over on
the damp earth.

A sense of calamity struck him with the force of a
blow. He crouched, paralyzed, beside the man he had
shot. Even when he rose, bringing up the rider's horse
and bending to lift the body and drape it across the
saddle, he could formulate no clear plan from the chaos
of his thoughts. He stepped back and slapped the animal
sharply across the rump. Then he stood, suddenly aware
of the night's deep chill, as the horse disappeared down
the trail, carrying its grisly burden.

CHAPTER VII

Will Roman rode into Judith City an hour before midnight. But for the lights of the hotel and bar, of Sid Patterson's saloon across the way, and the single lantern in front of Jess Logan's stable farther down, the brief length of the street was dark. As he reined in before the hotel he noticed a single horse standing at the rack in front of Sid's place. He stepped down, entering the hotel. Through the archway he saw two strangers, men in city clothes who looked like drummers, standing in idle conversation at the bar. Ruby Ferguson came out of the kitchen, meeting Will at the threshhold of the small dining room beyond the lobby. As if nervous, she tucked a stray wisp of hair into the bun at the nape of her neck. She said, "You alone? I thought you'd be riding out with—"

Will shook his head. "No sign of Dusty yet?"

"No." An expression of puzzled interest stirred openly in her face. Ruby was a forthright woman, not one to deny herself the answer to any question out of mere politeness or tact. She said, "What about Hank Crawford, Will? Old Ben have different ideas on the matter?"

"Yes," Will said. "Different ideas, Ruby."

"Don't do anything foolish, Will. You know Ben. A man gets older, he gets caution in his blood. But he still holds the reins just the same."

He glanced at the stairs. Ruby said, "She turned in half an hour ago. I gave her the back bedroom, across from Ed's and mine. I'm glad you brought her in, Will. I can use her. She and the boy will get along here just fine."

He managed a smile. "You can tell her we'll take over

what stock she has left. At least she won't be completely broke." He turned toward the door.

"If Dusty comes in, what shall I tell him?"

"I'll be around."

He went outside, standing laxly on the walk, letting the problem of Laurie Carstairs and her two-year-old son occupy his mind for the length of time it took to roll a smoke. He stepped down then, angling across the street toward the lighted front of Sid Patterson's saloon. The horse at the rack before Sid's twitched its tail, craning its head around at his approach. Seeing the brand upon its hip, Will frowned. He stepped up to the walk and crossed it, pushing through the swinging batwing doors.

Two men stood at the bar, one near the front, the other well toward the back. Will nodded at Sheriff Lew Brady, who had been talking to Patterson at the far end. Then his attention centered upon the hunched shoulders and back of the lone customer closer at hand. He stopped beside the youth as Sid came up behind the bar with bottle and glass.

"Pretty late to be holding up the bar all by yourself, isn't it, Mark?" Will filled the youngest Engstrand's empty glass before he poured his own drink. "Mind if I join you?"

He lifted his drink before he saw the warning expression on Sid Patterson's rotund face. He glanced at Mark. The kid was drunk. Without acknowledging Roman's presence, Mark clutched the filled glass and gulped at it. A good half of the whisky slopped over the bar. Will took his own nip and laid a hand upon the young rider's shoulder.

"Never figured you for a toper, Mark. Trying to make up for lost time?"

Mark Engstrand pushed himself back from the bar, staggering slightly as he shrugged free of Will's hand. Mark had turned twenty this past year, but his smooth, sullen features belied the fact. Will noticed that he had trouble focusing his eyes.

"Sure. Makin' up for lost time. Why not? Any damn business a'yours?"

The boy was wearing a sixgun. Will knew Mark had owned a gun for some time, but he also knew Mark seldom carried it. Since childhood in Texas, Mark had been shy of guns and gunplay of any kind. He'd always had to be forced to accompany his older brothers on their occasional hunting trips.

"Didn't mean to be too curious," Will said easily. "Any man's got a right to pin one on if he feels like it. Only there's no need to drink alone." He paused and added, "Not having trouble at home?"

"Any man, eh?" Mark ignored Will's last words, clutching at the bar as he weaved unexpectedly upon his feet. "But not a squirt like me. That what you mean?"

Roman waited, hoping this would pass. Something serious was eating upon Mark, something that might very well be connected with Hank Crawford's death and the burning of the Carstairs place earlier tonight. He wondered how long Mark had been in town.

Lew Brady moved along the length of the bar.

"Looks to me like you've had about enough, sonny boy." The sheriff made an attempt at joviality. "Might be a good idea if you hit out for home."

Mark swung about abruptly, his spurs rattling as his bootheels jarred against the floor. He stuck his chin out at Brady.

"Had enough, eh? Damn it, Fatbelly, I'll let you know when I've had enough!"

Mark reached for the shiny grip of his pistol. Roman stepped in, grasping Mark's wrist before the weapon came clear of its holster. With a rising, twisting motion he pried the gun free, breaking it and emptying the shells upon the floor. Mark glared at him from a face suddenly gone crimson.

"Sorry, Mark. But I think the sheriff's right." Roman extended the pistol, grip foremost. "Mind if I ride out a ways with you?"

For the space of several seconds Mark Engstrand stared at Will. Then he cursed, a single, foul and bitter word. He ignored the weapon in Roman's hand and strode quickly from the saloon. Outside he grasped the mount's reins and lurched into the saddle, swinging rapidly down the street and out of town.

Shame and frustration choked Mark Engstrand as he rode blindly for home. There was hatred and bitterness in him too, and a knowledge of his own weakness that was almost unbearable to stand. Sobering as he rode, he once more had visions of the flaming cabin and barn; he saw Hank Crawford stiffen beneath the impact of bullets fired by his father's and eldest brother's hands. He crossed the river bridge above town. He saw three men ride out of the darkness before him. His first impulse was to ride uncaring past the trio, but then he heard his father's voice lift in harsh command. He reined down at once, hearing Jere's contemptuous bark of laughter directly ahead.

"Well, well. So the strayed lamb is found. Been gettin' your feet warm with a bottle, laddie?"

Sam Engstrand said, "Who's in town, boy? Roman or Brady get up a posse yet?" When Mark did not answer he reined closer, adding, "Speak up, damn it! You been shootin' off your face to that woman-chasin' ramrod? Son or no son, I'll take a horsewhip to—"

"No." Mark forced the word through clenched teeth. "I ain't been shootin' off my face and I don't give a damn what you do. You can all go to hell, for all I care."

Jere's laugh came again, but it was Matt who spoke now.

"It might be all right at that, Pa, if Mark's been in town since he ran out on us at the Carstairs place. He could swear we was all to home when he rode into town, was anybody to ask."

Hatred and fear crouched side by side in Mark Engstrand's soul. All his life he had hated and feared these three who were his own father and brothers. Sam Engstrand cleared his throat gruffly.

"All right, boy. Light out for home. But remember what your brother said. I'd whip you down till you couldn't walk if you got any smart ideas about tellin' anybody what happened tonight, understand?"

Mark sank spur to his mount, fleeing the ridicule and

contempt of his older brother's laughter which pursued
him through the bitter night.

Will Roman idled his second drink on Sid Patterson's
bar, frowning absently at the damp circles it made on
the polished plank. He glanced into the mirror, irritated
by Lew Brady's obsequious tone. He shook his head at
the fat sheriff's reflection in the glass.

"You're supposed to be the law around here," he said.
"It's not up to me to tell you what to do."

Brady's eyes narrowed within their sagging pouches.
He poured himself a drink.

"That's all right for you to say," he said mildly. "You're
foreman of Box and I'm sheriff on the Judith. But you
know damned well it's the old man who's got the say-so.
Ain't neither one of us goin' to move a finger, 'less Ben
gives the word."

It was nothing but the truth and Will had no reply.
Brady tossed off his drink, wiping his mustaches with
the back of his hand.

"Course," he continued, "I can't say but what I agree
with old Ben at that. Could be he's right about the
rustlin' and all bein' the work of that bunch as was run
out of Miles here a while back. Anyway, I reckon I better
wait for the meetin' tomorrow night 'fore I make my
move."

The man's incompetence stirred annoyance in Roman.
He said, "The only strange riders around here are the
ones Frank Kessler hired lately. If you want something
to do, it might be a good idea to write the sheriff at
Miles and get what names and descriptions he's got."

"Say, now! That's a right smart idea at that!" The
sheriff slapped the rim of the bar as if such an obvious
procedure were a rare stroke of genius. He said loudly,
"I'll sure get that little thing done before I turn in
tonight! May just be I'll bust up this gang before they
get a foothold hereabouts!"

The foolishness of the statement touched Will's sense
of humor. He said, "Figure you'll ride up on the bench
and make the Kesslers trot out their boys when you've
heard from Miles City?"

Brady frowned, as though he suspected Roman of pulling his leg. He took on a truculent air.

"You can laugh," he said, "but I reckon I can deputize me enough gents to make it stick, if I have to. I may be fat and gettin' on, but by damn I'm wearin' this badge fair and legal."

Will's amusement faded as the sheriff left the saloon. Perhaps Brady might prove himself to be made of sterner stuff than anyone figured. However, such an event was more than unlikely. Whisky talked loud in a man, but helped little when the time came to act. Roman took his drink. Checking the clock above the backbar he felt a renewed stab of anxiety. What was keeping Dusty?

The plopping of hoofs in the muddy street outside drew him away from the bar. He pushed open the batwings and stepped out to the walk just as the three Engstrands reined up at the rack before the saloon. The surprise on both sides was mutual. In the outthrown light from the bar, Sam Engstrand's heavy features set instantly into a scowl. His face was puffed and discolored from the beating Roman had given him. Jere and Matt Engstrand grew tense, their eyes narrowed alertly.

Will was the first to speak.

"You weren't looking for me by any chance, were you, Sam?"

For a moment none of the Engstrands spoke. Then Sam cursed, spitting deliberately into the mud between rack and walk.

"When I come lookin' for you, mister, you won't have time to ask."

He stepped down, looping his mount's reins on the rail.

Roman said, "Reckon there's no need asking if you picked up Carstairs' trail."

Sam stepped up to the walk, his two sons cautiously following suit.

"Ain't nothing stoppin' you asking," Sam said. "But gettin' an answer's another thing."

Engstrand started toward the swinging doors. Roman moved into his path. Engstrand drew up, shoulders bunching beneath his sheepskin coat.

"I'm asking," Roman said quietly, "and I'm expecting an answer."

Sam Engstrand glanced sidelong at his two sons. Will was sure Engstrand would not allow himself to be provoked into open action, and he found himself regretting that this was so. Something must have happened to Dusty. Otherwise, why had he not arrived in town before the Engstrands? These were not the three whom he and Dusty had sighted below the Carstairs place, but he thrust the fact aside.

He said, "Hank Crawford was a good man. A damned good man, Sam. Somebody's going to hang over this little deal."

The shade of cunning that had crept into Engstrand's battered face faded abruptly. For an instant Will thought he detected a gleam of apprehension in the big man's eyes. Then Sam shook his head.

"You're on the wrong track if you think you can pin that little sortie on me and my boys," he said. "Sure, I heard about it. My young 'un, Mark, was here in town and he give us the word a few minutes ago. Too bad about Hank and the Carstairs place, though I can't say I'm wastin' any tears over the last." He paused, measuring Will shrewdly. "You may not know it, ramrod, but you're walkin' on pretty thin ice these days. Me and your boss had a nice little talk about you this mornin'."

The truth of this assertion lit a momentary flicker of anger in Will. But then a single horseman swung into the street, drawing his attention away. The lone rider had come into town from the west and for several seconds Roman weighed his next move. If Dusty brought the proof he needed, Jere Engstrand was the man to watch in case of an open break.

A moment later the oncoming rider swung past the recently lighted front of Lew Brady's office. It was not Dusty Wilson, but Reno Sinclair. Reno paused before the hotel, then came on, reining up beside the Engstrand mounts. His habitual grin flashed at sight of Will.

"Ain't breakin' in on a private party, am I, boy?" He seemed cautious in spite of his smile. "Me, I'm dry as a boneyard and twice as dead. Next time the old man wants a messenger boy I'll let you handle the job."

Controlling his impatience, Will said, "Didn't see any sign of Dusty while you were making the rounds?"

Reno shook his head. His glance took in the Engstrands, coming to rest on Sam.

"If I'd known you were riding into town this late, Sam," he said, "it would have saved me the trip out to your place to tell you about the meeting tomorrow night at Box." He shrugged and stepped down from the saddle. "Hell, nobody cares if a man rides his tail off."

Will Roman chewed his lip, faintly aware of some undercurrent he could not quite pin down. Reno had said that so deliberately, like an actor in a play. Why?

He said, "You rode out to Chair tonight and Sam and his boys were there?"

"Sure," Reno said. "I hit Sam's place first, then made the rounds. Figured somebody else could get the word up to Kesslers' tomorrow. Me, I'm done." He winked archly at Will. "Hell, you heard Ben lay down the law to me, boy."

For Will, the whole thing rang hollow. And yet, after all, why would Reno say the Engstrands had been home if they hadn't? Of course, they would have had time to circle back to their home place after killing Hank and burning the Carstairs cabin. But the three he and Dusty had intercepted had been heading south toward the KK spread. Roman studied Sam Engstrand, seeing the bare suggestion of a smile on his heavy, bruised features.

"Something wrong with a man eatin' supper on his own place, ramrod?" Sam asked, and turned to Reno. "Your sidekick's got the idea me and my boys blasted Crawford and burned out the Carstairs place. You figure the same?"

Rena looked uncomfortable. He said, "Me, I've got the Slash D to worry about. I figure that's enough for right now." His full, handsome face flushed as he met Will's eye. "Damn it, you boys voted yourself in a sheriff!" he said hotly. "I say let him earn his pay!"

Roman smiled thinly. "You really mean that, don't you, Reno?"

He did not wait for an answer. He cut across the street at an angle toward the hotel. He had not reached the opposite walk when he heard a yell from the street's far end. Next, he saw a man run out of Jess Logan's stable, clutching for the bridle of a riderless horse in the glow of the single lantern.

Without quite understanding his own urgency, Will began running that way. The man ahead, whom he recognized now as Jess Logan, had got a grip on the nervously shying horse. As Logan called out once more, Roman saw a figure lying sprawled in the mud in front of the stable. He did not need to be told that this man had slipped from the saddle of the skittish mount, and after a few more strides he knew who the man was.

Dusty Wilson had returned to Judith City.

CHAPTER VIII

Doc Trimble was a small man with a sharp pinched face and eyes magnified owlishly by the square-cut lenses of a pince-nez he wore clamped to the thin, humped bridge of his nose. He stepped from the room into the hall and pulled the door shut behind him. He placed a round bowler hat squarely upon his head, then bobbed the head at Will and Laurie Carstairs.

"It's a bad wound," he said precisely. "He might live. He might not. We should know by morning." His owl eyes briefly contemplated the faded robe Laurie wore over her nightdress. "Perhaps it would be a good idea if you got what sleep you could, Mrs. Carstairs. Mrs. Ferguson will sit up with the patient the first few hours. He has not regained consciousness and perhaps he never will. You may call me if he seems to take a turn for the worse."

The doctor minced along the hallway and went down the stairs. Laurie touched Will's arm. Her hair lay in two heavy braids down her back. Her face was pale, her eyes worried.

"You shouldn't blame yourself, Will," she said softly. "Dusty would be the last one to want that."

Will spread his hands and let them drop.

"You need sleep," Laurie told him. "Ruby or I will call you if there's any change."

He had picked Dusty Wilson up in his arms and brought him to the hotel. He had been numb with shock, and yet both guilt and a lust for vengeance stirred beneath the numbness. He must. . . . But no, what she said was true. There was no sense in blaming himself for what had happened to Dusty. He, Will Roman, had sent the little tophand off against overwhelming odds, and he must square it somehow. Later, though. Later. He smiled at Laurie.

"You heard the doctor, Mrs. Carstairs," he said. "You'd better hit that pillow, or you'll fall asleep on the job."

She continued to search his face. She lifted a hand, touching the line of his jaw. Then, as though belatedly realizing what she had done, she drew back, her eyes widening.

Roman swallowed at something sticky in his throat.

"Will it ever be different, Will Roman?" She asked the question without emotion, as though she had withdrawn from herself and was not personally involved. "Is it beyond everyone's power to control their own lives? Do we just live day to day at the mercy of something we know nothing about?"

There was no answer in him and he gave her none.

She said, "You're in love with her, aren't you? The girl Reno married." She did not wait for an answer, but squeezed his arm lightly. "Please, Will. Try to sleep." She was gone then, moving along the hall to her own room at the rear.

After a moment Roman went to the stairs. Reno Sinclair stood on the landing, leaning against the rail. Reno walked beside him down the remaining steps.

"It's the Kesslers, Will. I'd stake my life on that."

Roman came to a stand at the bottom. The years he had shared with Reno, the War and the hard years since, flickered and were gone from his mind.

"Was a time," he said, "when that's all you had to stake. Maybe you'd be smart to play something cheaper now."

He walked away from Sinclair. He went into the bar. Ed Ferguson whisked bottle and glass onto the counter and backed off. Lew Brady came down the bar to Will. The two drummers stood near the far end, casting curious glances at the two men.

"Figure there's any sense in gittin' up a posse, Will?" The sheriff looked worried, his eyes following the movement of Roman's hands as Will poured and took down a swift drink. "Maybe I better ride out and see Ben?"

Will did not speak. He took a second drink, pulled out

tobacco and papers and rolled himself a smoke. He in-
haled deeply, pouring the glass full once more.

"Well, good Lord, Will—" Brady's grimace of distress
creased the deep flesh of his cheeks. "Somethin' sure
ought'a be done. After all, I'm sheriff and—"

"Why don't you go to hell, Lew?"

Though spoken mildly, the words seemed to slash
across the room's silence. Brady turned brick red. He
opened his mouth, noticed the drummers watching him,
and strode heavily from the room.

One of the drummers laughed. Roman looked at him
and the drummer sputtered to a stop. Will tossed down
his third drink.

Ten minutes later he left the bar. Whisky did not help.
It was the waiting, the not knowing whether Dusty would
live or die, and the knowledge of his own helplessness,
that bore ruthlessly upon him now. He had gone over
and over the question of the identity of the three men
Dusty had trailed. Neither of the Kesslers could possibly
have been at such a place at that particular time, because
he and Dusty had seen both the brothers up on the bench
only a few hours ago. If not the Kesslers, who else?

Stepping out to the street, Roman saw that Reno's
mount was gone from the rack in front of Patterson's
Saloon. The three Engstrand horses, however, stood idly
together. What about Reno's story that Sam and his boys
had been home when he had stopped by with word of
the meeting at Box tomorrow night? It would have been
ten o'clock by the time Reno reached Chair. Plenty of
time for the Engstrands to swing back north after shaking
Dusty. . . . If they had merely shaken Dusty.

He cut the thought. He'd get nowhere if he went over
there to confront Sam and his sons. What good were
accusations, even threats, without some kind of proof,
something a man could know and act upon fully? Ben,
at least, was right to that extent.

Roman entered the lobby and mounted the stairs. The
aftertaste of the whisky was foul in his mouth as he un-
dressed in the darkness of his room and crawled in bed.
He lay awake a long time, and then he slept.

It was barely light outside when Will awoke. He washed and dressed quickly, then hurried down the hall to Dusty's room. He eased the door open.

The lamp still burned on a table. Laurie Carstairs sat in a chair beside the bed, weary but awake. Dusty lay quietly, his two-colored hair awry against the white pillow, his chest barely moving the blanket as he breathed.

Laurie rose. She pushed Will gently into the hall, pulling the door to behind her. Her eyes were darkly shadowed as she looked up at him.

"I don't know, Will," she said. "He's been breathing irregularly the past hour or so. Perhaps you'd better get the doctor."

He nodded, and then he astonished himself.

"She married Reno," he said.

Laurie blinked, bewildered. Then she understood, and color flooded her cheeks. He did not press the matter. He walked down the hall toward the stairs.

Doc Trimble and his wife lived in a small house near the river, a hundred yards beyond the town's street. Returning to the hotel with the doctor, Will heard Ruby call from the kitchen, so he went in. She set steaming coffee and a large breakfast of ham, eggs and fried potatoes before him. She was fully dressed, though her hair, as usual, seemed to defy her efforts to keep it neatly coiled upon her neck. Taking a chair at the table, she watched him eat for several moments before she spoke.

"It's not my affair, Will," she said, "but I've got an idea that before this thing's over you're going to run into Jack Carstairs, big as life. Have you thought what you're going to do then?"

Will tried silence, but it didn't stop Ruby.

She said, "I'm a woman and I know how women feel about these things. Jack's no good and never was. But you'd better not be the one to kill him. She'd never forgive you for it, Will. She couldn't. I know."

Will drank the last of his coffee and got up. He said, "You're taking a hell of a lot for granted, Ruby. Maybe you'd better stick to running your hotel."

Unabashed, she followed him to the kitchen door.

"You think it's still this high and mighty gal Reno married, eh? Don't fool yourself, Will. And remember what I said about Jack. If it's got to be done, there are plenty others who'd jump at the chance of swinging that boy."

He strode through the small dining room to the lobby. The two traveling men were coming down the stairs and Will heard Jeb Wakeley's voice lash out at his team as he brought the stage up from the livery stable and halted before the hotel. Upstairs, the doctor said Dusty's condition was still uncertain. Roman went down to Jess Logan's stable. He saddled the gelding and rode out of town.

At Box, Roman found Reno Sinclair and four of his own men stepping to saddle in the open yard. The line riders nodded or spoke their greetings, but Reno's usual grin wasn't forthcoming. Will caught himself thinking that Reno's jovial manner had been a pretty forced thing since he had returned to the Judith.

He said, "Figure on taking every hand I've got?"

Reno swung astride his mount, taking his time about it.

"You know damned well I've got to get that cut made before she starts to blow," he said. "The old man gave me the nod on taking the rest of the boys."

"That cut means a lot to you, don't it, Reno?"

"You damned right it does," Reno said. "I aim to build Slash into one of the biggest spreads north of the Pecos and I'm not letting every two-bit rustler or incidental shooting stop me, either!"

"Incidental?" Will said. "Dusty's life is only incidental to you, Reno?"

Reno sat his horse like a statue, bereft of speech. Roman looked at his men.

"You boys cool your heels a bit," he said. "I'm making medicine with the old man."

He stepped down. One of the punchers came forward to take his mount. Reno suddenly found his voice.

"You men hit the saddle! Damn it, I've got a job to do!"

From the ranch house porch, Ellen called, "Reno, what is it? Oh—Will—"

Roman said, "Set easy, boys. I'll give you the word. That's an order." Then he crossed the yard to the house, meeting Ellen as she came down the steps. She was wear-

ing a heavy, dark riding skirt and a white blouse that
caught the bright morning sunlight.

"Reno told us about Dusty," she began. "I'm so sorry,
Will. Is there anything—"

He answered her with a headshake, but passed her
without speaking. He entered the house. Amantha Fowler came toward him with outstretched arms. He held
her a moment, wondering at the seeming frailness of
these shoulders which had borne the years with such
astonishing strength.

"He's still living, Ma," he said quickly, knowing that
Amantha Fowler had taken both his friends to her heart
the day he brought them home after the War. "I came
to see Ben," he added, and she stiffened a little.

"You know best, Will. But, please, don't say anything
that—that you might regret later."

"I'll try," he said, and left her.

Ben Fowler was sitting upright in bed, having just finished his breakfast. His cheeks were white with stubble,
the folds of flesh beneath his jaw more slack than usual.
His hoary mane of hair still bristled, however, and after
a brief inquiry into Dusty's condition he tightened up.

"Don't say it, boy," he cautioned. "I know what's in
your mind. And my answer's the same as it was last
night. You're a little young to remember it, but I've been
through a couple of range wars and I know what they're
like. I say that keepin' the peace here on the Judith is
worth a lot of talk and a lot of trouble. A lot more than
you seem to be willin' to take right now."

Will started to speak. The old man cut him off with a
gesture.

"Sure, I know how you feel about Dusty. And about
Hank Crawford, far as that goes. I feel the same way and
somebody will pay. I promise you that. But just the same,
I'm holding that meetin' here tonight. We'll talk this
thing out and see what's to be done."

A coldness grew in the pit of Will's stomach. He said,
"I've never gone against you, Ben. But this is personal.
Dusty Wilson is the best friend I ever had."

Ben Fowler sighed.

"You're my boy, Will," he said carefully. "It's always

been that way and I hope it always will be. But if you walk out that door with the idea of busting things wide open here on the Judith, you'll be through on Box. If I have to, I'll put Reno on as foreman and let him run the whole shebang." He took a deep breath. "I don't have to tell you what that would mean to me."

It was there between them then. All the years he had known and loved Ben like a father passed fleetingly and dropped from Will's mind.

"I'll be in town," he said. "But if Dusty dies, it looks like you've hired yourself a new foreman."

He turned, seeing Ellen and Amantha Fowler in the doorway. He brushed past them. Ellen followed him, catching and stopping him when he reached the front room. She gripped his arm, shaking him.

"Will, you—" she stammered the words— "you don't mean it? You wouldn't step out and let Reno—" She blushed suddenly, making a new start. "None of this is because of us, is it? Because I married Reno instead of you?"

"If you think I'm stepping out just to let Reno take over, you're mistaken, Ellen. To tell you the truth, I doubt if Reno could—" This was not what he had meant to say. He let it go tiredly. "I'm sorry, Ellen. I have nothing to say beyond what I told Ben."

"Is this the way it's to end, then? Are you leaving me just to vent your spite over some shooting—"

"Leaving you?" he said. "Leaving you, Ellen? I had the impression that someone else did the leaving. Or doesn't a marriage license change anything?"

She fluttered her hands, then clasped them.

"It's just that I'm not too sure any more, Will," she whispered. "Did I make a mistake—a horrible mistake—for both of us?"

Will Roman examined the lovely, distraught face of this girl who had crushed his dreams with a letter, and he saw her fully, saw within her, saw how complete was her concern for herself alone. She didn't really care whether or not Dusty lived. She felt nothing approaching true love for either Reno or himself. She was pleading

prettily—pleading for another chance to go on being vain
and shallow and utterly selfish.

"You can't have the world, Ellen," he said. "But if you
did, you'd probably be looking for another to go with it
before the week was out."

A breath escaped her. She slapped him. Then she fled
down the hall to her room.

As Will turned to leave, the door opened. Reno stepped
inside. Roman smiled thinly at him.

He said, "I'll give Dusty your best, boy," and stepped
past Reno, crossing porch and yard to his mount. He
waved casually at the punchers who stood about the yard.
"Relax, boys. I've got an idea Reno's going to change his
mind about making that cut when he talks to Ben." He
stepped to the saddle and rode away from the ranch.

In town, he had barely dismounted before the hotel
when he saw Ruby Ferguson come to the door. The long
and searching look she gave him, utterly devoid of any
suggestion of warmth or welcome, stopped him short on
the walk.

"He's gone," she said. "Dusty's gone."

Bright midmorning sunshine bathed the street, and
Will Roman felt cold.

He wheeled about, striding across the street to the
sheriff's office. Five minutes later he reappeared upon the
street. He entered Newton's Mercantile, several doors
farther along. He came out of Newton's breaking a new
box of shells and stuffing the lightly oiled cartridges into
the pockets of his coat. He moved once more to the
gelding he had left standing in front of the hotel.

As he stepped into the saddle, Ruby Ferguson came to
the edge of the walk. Across the street, Lew Brady was
watching silently from the door of his office.

"Take care, Will," Ruby said.

Will Roman reined the leggy gelding about and rode
south out of town.

Laurie Carstairs looked accusingly at Ruby, and then
at Ed Ferguson, who was wolfing his mid-day meal at
the kitchen table.

"Why didn't you tell me?" she said. "Didn't you think

I had the right to know he'd returned? And why would
Will ride out alone? Where was he going?"

Neither Ruby nor Ed seemed able to answer, although
it had been Ed's words, dropped in the midst of casual
conversation, which gave Laurie her first hint of Will
Roman's return from Box and his subsequent departure
nearly two hours ago. Ed Ferguson ducked his head,
gulped the last of his coffee and hurriedly left the table.
Ruby sighed and turned from the sink, meeting the issue
squarely.

"To tell you the truth, I didn't see why you should be
worried about it, one way or the other." Ruby's tone was
not unkind, but completely candid. "As to his riding out
alone, I've got an idea that Will and old man Fowler can't
see eye-to-eye on what should be done. In fact, I wouldn't
be surprised if Will had quit his job altogether."

"Oh, no, Ruby, he wouldn't do that. Why, Will opened
this country. He—"

"And Dusty Wilson was Will Roman's best friend. Or
don't you think that means anything to a man like Will?"

Laurie stared at the older woman. Will Roman quit
Box? Without having been aware of it until now, Laurie
suddenly realized that the power of Box and Will Roman's
own personal strength had always seemed one and the
same to her. Of course everyone knew that Ben Fowler
owned the Boxed F brand, both here and in Texas, but
Will had opened the Judith to graze and settlement and
his position had never been questioned.

Then the fact of her own dependence on Will Roman
came home to Laurie. How many times had he stopped
by the house since Jack had left, bringing gifts of food
and making sure that she and her son were all right? It
was hard to picture Will Roman as a jobless man without
the security and power of Box behind him. But he was a
jobless man, a man alone.

Will is in danger, Laurie thought, and got up from
the table.

"He's gone after the men who killed Dusty and Hank
Crawford," she said.

Ruby shrugged. "Didn't you think he would?"

"But not alone! Not against—" She faltered.

"Yes?" Ruby prompted. "Against who, Laurie?"

"Oh, Ruby! He'll be killed!"

Very slowly, Ruby dried her already dry hands on her apron. She said, "What do you know about this, Laurie Carstairs? If you know who's behind this whole thing—"

"No. Oh, no, Ruby!" Laurie shook her head furiously. "It's only that, whoever they are, I feel somehow that Jack is involved—that maybe none of this would have happened if it hadn't been for Jack. And somehow, some way, I'm to blame. If only I hadn't married Jack. He wasn't really ready to settle down. He—"

Laurie's utter misery convinced Ruby Ferguson. She took Laurie into her arms.

"Now, now, child. I'm sure there's enough blame to go around without your trying to hog it all."

After a moment Laurie straightened.

"Will you look after Jimmy a while? I'll be back before dark."

Ruby's brow furrowed, her head tilting slightly awry. "Now, see here, young lady. If you've any idea of going after Will Roman—"

"No, Ruby. I wouldn't know where to look, nor what to say if I found him. But perhaps I might find Jack. I know he was involved in the rustling. Before he disappeared last spring he used to ride the hills for days at a time. He never told me where he had been, or who he had seen. But there must have been someone. He had money and—" Her voice trailed off, but she added quickly, "Jimmy's had his dinner. He should be asleep for at least two more hours. He really wouldn't be too much trouble."

"Oh, I can take care of the boy." Ruby dismissed the subject as if annoyed. Then she said gently, "It's Will, isn't it, girl—in spite of hell or high water?"

A faint flush lifted in Laurie's cheeks.

"I might warn you," Ruby continued, "you're not the only one who's been hurt. That high-and-mighty new wife of Reno Sinclair's put Will through the wringer like a worn out shirt."

"Please, Mrs. Ferguson, I—"

"All right, then, get on with you. You're probably right. If Jack's not dead already, he'll know who killed Olsen,

Crawford and Dusty Wilson. It might just be that you'll get by up on the bench where a man wouldn't stand a chance. But if you're not back by nightfall or shortly after, there'll be a posse camping on the Kesslers' doorstep if I have to head it myself!"

CHAPTER IX

Reno Sinclair kept his face straight, but he writhed inwardly as Ben Fowler talked. He and Ben were alone in the bedroom at Box, but Reno knew that Ben's voice carried clearly enough down the hall for Ellen to hear. He tried not to show his true feelings, yet he was building a sheer, unadulterated hatred for the old man.

"In case you don't know it, Sinclair," Fowler was saying, "running a ranch is a little different from pushing a herd up the trail. Fact is, I ain't made up my mind yet to give you the job. And if it wasn't for Ellen, damned if I'd even consider it."

Reno drew a careful breath, hoping irrelevantly that the old man's hip hurt him as much as he pretended. The smile he put on his face felt like a mask of caked mud.

"If that's the way you feel about it, Ben," he suggested, "let's forget about the whole thing. I'll go ahead with the cut. Ellen and I will get along."

If only he didn't want the job so badly! If only . . . but he had to be patient now. He fixed his mind on the day when Ben Fowler would go south. Not only would he have control of Ellen's Slash D stock; the whole Montana Box would be in his grasp. Ben's expression clouded again with pain and anger and Reno forced these thoughts aside, taking no chance that Ben might perceive their direction.

Less than an hour ago Doc Trimble had arrived to have a look at Ben's hip. He had brought with him the news of Dusty's death and had mentioned Will's subsequent departure from town. Even now, Ben was still struggling

90

to keep his word about firing Will and putting Reno in his place, and Reno knew it.

"Yes, you'll get along!" the old man burst out. "Just like you always have—on the backs of those around you!"

Reno's smile faded altogether. Fortunately, Ellen chose that moment to appear in the open door. Ben's glare dropped to the faded patchwork quilt upon the bed. Maybe he was being unfair in venting his anger at Will on another man. In the next second he recanted. Damn it, Reno wasn't good enough for Will Roman's job! His head snapped up and he freshened his glare on Ellen.

"All right," he barked. "Your man's running the place. But under my direct orders and only until we see how things work out. Now get out of here, both of you!"

Reno turned, bent on a quick escape, but Ben wasn't through.

"And I'll hold you responsible for seeing that every man-jack who's running a head of stock in this basin is here at Box tonight!" Ben said. "Any man not here will be suspect and you can tell them that for me!"

Reno kept on going. Ellen ran after him, stopping him in the kitchen.

"Reno, please." The blueness of her eyes seemed to have turned a purple hue. "I'm sorry about Dad, Reno. You know how he is. But it's not that I wanted to talk to you about." She hesitated, then plunged on. "I want you to go after Will. Please, Reno, don't say no. I know you're angry and I don't blame you. But—I'm afraid, darling. He might be killed!"

Reno took his time, inspecting this girl he had married. His grin unfurled crookedly.

"What's the matter, old girl? Been thinking it over? Figure you made a mistake in your choice of a husband?"

"You know that isn't true, Reno!"

"Do I?" He watched her, watched her squirm and try not to show it. Finally he said, "Sure, I'll go after him. I'll bring him back to you all safe and sound—when the snow's ten feet deep on the Pecos and you can slide from here to there downhill."

He let it sink in, and then he walked through the back door. His sense of satisfaction had faded by the time he had given one of the men orders to ride out and call in the crew who were busy making the cut of Slash D stock from the Boxed F herds. And by the time he was in the saddle, heading toward town, he felt awful.

At the ford of the Judith he reined up, allowing his mount a brief drink. Staring sightlessly across the wide, shallow stream at the fringe of alder, willow and massive cottonwood, he admitted that his appointment as foreman of Box didn't help at all, so far as either the Kesslers or Sam Engstrand were concerned.

He had been a fool to tell Will that he had called at the Engstrand ranch to deliver Ben's summons. It had been an impulsive, spur-of-the-moment statement fashioned out of an anxiety to establish his own whereabouts at the time Dusty had been shot. He had known, of course, that Sam Engstrand would gladly back his word. Sam could use that lie to stay clear of guilt in the Crawford killing.

The trouble was, Sam Engstrand now had a hold on him.

Sam and his boys had not killed Dusty Wilson. If the murder were definitely pinned on someone else, then Sam would be free to bring pressure on Reno Sinclair, to blackmail him at will. This threat, added to the stranglehold Frank and Dobe Kessler already held about his neck, had kept Reno sleepless at Box, and it tortured him now. Whatever his boys might be, Sam Engstrand was no fool. That he had heard the shot which had dropped Dusty Wilson from the saddle was certain. Perhaps he and his boys had waited beside the trail and discovered Dusty's body draped over the saddle of his mount before they rode on into town. In any case, by volunteering false information Reno had given himself away to Sam.

Undoubtedly Sam had correctly interpreted the motive behind Reno's lie. Yet Reno had to be sure. Too, there was the fact of the Engstrand's presence upon KK range. This in itself was proof of their guilt in Hank Crawford's murder. The pot could not very well call the kettle black, but he would have to see Sam before the meeting tonight. Spurring directly across the stream, he swung off the road to town, heading northwest at a lope.

The sun was slanting across the tree-shaded yard when he rode into Chair. Jere and Matt Engstrand got up from the porch as he stopped in front of the house. Jere's expression was plainly contemptuous as he eyed Reno.

"Hey, Pal" he called. "We in the market for any alibis today?"

Reno reminded himself that Jere Engstrand would have to be taken down a few notches one of these days. Then Sam pushed open the screen door and stepped out on the porch. The bruises on his face had darkened, giving him a sinister air. Reno nodded without stepping down.

"Figured I'd ride by and remind you of the meeting at Box tonight," he said.

Shirtless, his arms and upper body clad in filthy woolen underwear, Sam Engstrand hooked his thumbs beneath broad suspenders, teetering from heel to toe as he eyed Reno Sinclair from the edge of the porch. Sam was unarmed, but Reno noticed that Jere and Matt fingered their sixguns as they lounged, seemingly languid, upon either side of the steps. He felt very uncomfortable.

"Why, now," Sam said finally, "I reckon that's right considerate of you, neighbor. Seems to me, in fact, you been leanin' over backwards to do us a good turn here lately. Could be we ought to get together a little more—seein' you're starting up on your own these days."

Reno did not miss Sam's tone of studied and cynical humor, or the grins on the faces of Jere and Matt.

He said, "A little more than that, Sam. I'm taking over Box, as of today."

This information cut through their cynicism. He had their full attention now and he would be wise to exploit it.

"Roman's through," he said. "But that doesn't mean he can't rake up trouble and plenty of it. You know and I know pretty well all that happened last night. Will's on the warpath. He may not know much but he suspects plenty. And someone's going to pay through the nose."

Engstrand rubbed a tentative hand along his jaw. "And who do you figure this someone's goin' to be?"

"It won't be me. And if you're smart, Sam, it won't be you."

Engstrand's eyebrow lifted quizzically. "If I'm smart, eh?" Again the taunting grin apeared. "I'd say you'd better be the smart one, Sinclair. You're walkin' a mighty fine line and if I was to get the notion I reckon I could topple you off most any time."

The truth of these words, as well as the sure manner in which they were spoken, touched off a spasm of apprehension in Reno. Sam did hold the upper hand.

Reno said hotly, "Killing Crawford put you pretty far out on a limb, Sam. Don't forget I'm ramming Box now. It might pay you to step easy. Understand?"

Sam lowered his head like a bull ready to charge. Off to one side, Jere Engstrand straightened slightly, hitching his gunbelt. But then Sam relaxed, and the mocking humor came back.

"Case of you scratch my back and I'll scratch yours, and to hell with Frank and Dobe—eh, Sinclair?" Sam chuckled. "Well, it might work out, at that. We'll see what happens up on the bench." He started to turn, but looked back at Reno once more.

"Reckon you know it was Frank and Dobe busted Carstairs loose. If things fall down around Frank, he might let Jack talk just for laughs. You, now—you wouldn't have anything to worry about if that happened, would you, Sinclair?"

Reno couldn't suppress a visible wince. Engstrand laughed. With one hand extended to open the door, he said, "Sure. With you in the saddle at Box, it could be we'll get along just fine, boy. Things might look a lot different here on the Judith. We'll see."

Reno rode on toward town. The threat had been plain enough, God knew. It ate at him. Suddenly, as he came within sight of town, desperation welled up in Reno so strongly that he felt physically sick. Instead of achieving independent security and freedom upon marrying Ellen and coming north, he had gotten himself hemmed in on every hand: by the Kesslers, with their threat to expose him unless he continued the rustling he had foolishly started; by Sam Engstrand over the matter of Dusty; by old Ben's dislike and distrust. . . .

Abruptly, an idea struck him, a solution so profound

and satisfying that he unconsciously drew back on the reins. Staring off across the rolling land toward the haze of rising hills in the distance, he thought how simple the whole thing would be. Why, Ellen was sure to inherit Box! And he, Reno Sinclair, instead of being a mere foreman-on-parole, so to speak, could control Ellen and Box.

He could, if Ben were out of the way.

Reno Sinclair felt the need for whisky. For quantities of whisky. He touched spur to his horse's flanks and covered the remaining mile into town at a run.

Lying prone on the ridge directly above Frank Kessler's KK headquarters, Will Roman shifted his position slightly to avoid the sharp edge of a rock beneath his hip. Once more he adjusted the battered binoculars and searched the country beyond the outjutting ridge off to his right. For a full hour he had watched the ranch, without cutting sign of the man he sought.

Jack Carstairs was the key to the whole situation here on the Judith. Will had started out hot after an open showdown with Sam Engstrand and the Kesslers, but the ride up to the bench had cooled his rage. He needed proof before he braced those men. He needed Jack Carstairs.

For a while he had watched Frank Kessler and two of the gun-handy riders he and Dusty had noticed yesterday, expecting others to join them. No one did, and he prepared to leave, intending to drop down to the cabin on the far side of the southerly ridge. Then he had seen Dobe ride in from that direction. The younger Kessler had disappeared inside the house ten minutes ago. Now, impatient once more, Roman started to rise. Just as he moved, he noticed a single rider at the far edge of the meadow below the house.

He readjusted his glasses. The double lenses brought the scene below leaping into sudden focus. He drew a quick breath of surprise tinged with disbelief. Yet there could be no mistake. The oncoming rider, crossing the open meadow with no attempt at concealment, was Laurie Carstairs.

Roman felt the urge to shout, to rise and wave her

away from the place. Beyond doubt, the Kesslers had recruited their hardcase crew from the ranks of the rustler gang which had been operating around Miles City. Regardless of where Sam Engstrand stood, Frank and Dobe Kessler had stepped across the line of the law. At the very least, they had killed Lew's deputy the night they broke Jack Carstairs out of jail, after putting in a profitable year rustling several hundred head of basin stock.

Yet as he rose now, seeing Laurie draw up in front of the house below, Will realized that nothing less than a gunshot would attract her attention. And, very likely, not even a shot would swerve her from whatever purpose had brought her to the bench. Helpless to aid her, he saw several men step out of the house into the yard.

Both Kessler brothers were in the group and some sort of argument seemed to be taking place. Laurie, sitting straight in the saddle, shook her head as the gnarled, stooped Frank Kessler waved his arms in unheard expostulation. Roman was upon the verge of moving back to his mount on the timbered ridge when he saw Laurie clutch at her belt. Her hand came out gripping a heavy pistol.

Standing stiffly on the knoll, Will watched the others closely. He wished to God he had his carbine here, but even so the distance was too great for any accuracy. One of the hired gun hands stepped slightly forward. Will saw Frank's sudden gesture and the puncher's resulting shrug. He saw Dobe shake his head obstinately, as though at some word of Frank's. Only when Dobe mounted his horse and headed out toward the foot of the ridge, with Laurie trailing along in his wake, did Will draw a deep breath of relief.

Somehow, Laurie Carstairs had managed, at least temporarily, to gain her way. Will left the crest of the knoll, slipping back to where he had left his horse. As he rode off to the south beneath the concealing timber his first supposition—that Laurie had ridden into the hills on his own trail—struck him as both pretentious and false. She had come in search of her husband, of course. And, regardless of his later plans for the girl, Frank Kessler had decided to let her see Jack.

Passing the junction of the outjutting ridge with the higher slope, Will caught a glimpse of the small cabin he and Dusty had visited the day before. It would take half an hour for Dobe Kessler and Laurie to circle the timbered spur and approach the tiny meadow in which the cabin stood. Dropping down the long descent through the pines, he wished he and Dusty had forced the issue yesterday when they had the chance. Laurie's presence was going to be more of a handicap than a help within the next hour.

Dismounting above a clump of screening aspen, he moved carefully down the steep slope. Circling off to his right to avoid a low but crumbling shelf directly behind the log cabin, he gained the flat midway between the shack and the nearby creek. There was no sign of smoke at the chimney, nor had Laurie and Dobe Kessler yet reached the meadow beyond. For an instant Roman feared his calculations had been wrong. Perhaps the Kesslers had moved Carstairs and he was merely wasting his time.

As he eased along the foot of the slope he caught sight of an unsaddled horse beneath the small lean-to against the cabin's near wall. It was the same animal he had seen here yesterday. At least, he mused, the gunman named Bert would be somewhere about the place. He stepped out carefully, heading for the windowless rear wall of the cabin. The tethered horse whinnied in sudden fright. Will did not wait. He darted into the space between the low bluff and the cabin's rear wall.

Roman cursed inwardly. He didn't want trouble with that gunhawk now. If he were forced into gunplay before Dobe and Laurie Carstairs arrived, the consequences might be terrible. Dobe wouldn't hesitate to use Laurie as a hostage.

He reached the cabin's far corner. He heard the chink of rowels on hard earth and knew that Bert had stepped outside to investigate the noise. He turned, facing back the way he had come, in case the man should step past the lean-to stable. Then Dobe Kessler's voice hailed the cabin from the meadow.

Bert answered the call. Will heard the sound of horses drawing up in front of the cabin. He peered around the corner, then moved forward, stopping just short of the front wall.

"Say, now," the gunman called Bert said with relish, "this is more like it. Man gets downright lonesome up here in these hills. Aimin' to leave her with us, are you, Dobe?"

"Not likely." Dobe's gruff tones gave answer. "You, in there! Carstairs! Got a visitor for you if you think you can stand it. Step out."

"Carstairs' missus, eh?" the gunman marveled. "Now I sure never—"

The man's words cut off. He stood open mouthed as Roman stepped into the clear from the cabin's far corner. Will, sizing up the situation instantly, cursed the chance which placed Dobe Kessler directly beyond Laurie's mounted figure.

But the girl kept on looking at her husband in the open doorway. She had not seen Will. She stepped down, speaking Jack's name, and Dobe saw Roman for the first time. He yelled at Bert and clawed for his sixgun.

Roman shouted, "Drop, Laurie!" and his hand swept up, clearing the gun from his holster. Laurie spun about, utterly confused.

Roman fired as his weapon came up, hardly conscious of the explosion of Kessler's gun and the nearness of the bullet that sang past his head. Dobe yelled once, a barking, startled cry that cut off as quickly as it was uttered. His gun dropped to earth and he sagged, slipping all at once from the saddle. Roman heard Laurie's quick cry of protest and turned that way.

Jack had run out of the open door, clutching at the gun Laurie still held in her hand. His rush had put him directly between Roman and the gunman Bert. As Will turned the gunman fired.

Carstairs spun about as though struck by some gigantic but unseen force. He stumbled and Bert's second shot took him squarely in the back. Again Roman yelled at the girl as he darted off to one side to get her out of the line of fire.

The gunhand made a turn as though to run for cover. But as Roman drew into the clear Bert's eyes widened, fear showing upon the bearded lines of his face. He was caught that way, on half-balance, when Will called his name. Bert fired wildly and Roman killed him as he would have shot a wolf, aiming deliberately and taking his time. Bert was dead before his body struck earth.

Returning his weapon to holster, Will glanced down at the man near his feet. In circling away from Laurie and Jack he had almost stumbled across the body of Dobe Kessler. The rancher's arms were spread wide as he stared sightlessly at the sky, one leg bent grotesquely beneath the other.

Laurie was kneeling beside her husband. Holding his head and shoulders upright, she bent her own head as if she were listening to his words. Will went over to them. He saw Jack's eyes turn up to his face. Jack Carstairs' thin, handsome face was drawn with pain. His mouth worked spasmodically, as though he could not utter the words he sought to speak. Without warning, blood welled up in his mouth, spilling down over his chin in a dark viscous flood. His eyes rolled back and his body went limp in Laurie's arms.

Will stood beside the girl without movement or speech. She lowered Jack's body slowly and got to her feet. There was blood upon her hands and clothes, but she did not seem to notice this fact. She turned, staring off across the sunlit meadow.

"I killed him," she said dully. "He tried to take my gun to kill that man. I was confused. I wouldn't let go."

"No." Will did not attempt to touch her, or offer his sympathy in any way. He said, "I'm afraid Jack committed suicide a long while ago." Leaving her there, he went to the lean-to and led the dead gunman's mount into the yard. He lashed the bodies of Bert and Dobe across the animal's back and bound Jack Carstairs to Dobe Kessler's mount. Then he returned to Laurie.

She had not moved, and he saw no sign of tears in her eyes as they came slowly into focus upon his face. She seemed to drift back to reality from some unknown region beyond.

"Yes," she whispered softly. "We have to go on, don't we? The living must live and—" Her voice trailed off, as though she had neither the energy nor interest to continue. Roman steeled himself to speak.

"Did Jack say anything before he died?" he asked. "It might be important, Laurie. Did he say anything at all?"

The girl merely stared at him, the gray depths of her eyes seemingly without emotion of any kind. Roman's jaw tightened but he did not press the point. He told her to wait and went up the short slope to his own saddled mount. He had no way of knowing the extent of shock she had suffered, but he felt bleak as he stepped up to the saddle and reined back down the short grade.

Surprisingly, she had caught and mounted her own horse and was waiting for him beside the other two animals with their grisly burdens. Her eyes seemed less blank, though there was little in her but acquiescence as he outlined his plan. She objected to nothing except his suggestion that she return alone to Judith City.

"No," she said dully, "I'll stay with you." Though her expression remained unchanged, she added suddenly, "You know he didn't do it, don't you? Jack had no part in killing Sheriff Brady's deputy. It was Frank and Dobe Kessler. Jack was working for them. He said Frank knew you would suspect Sam Engstrand. He said—"

Once more her voice trailed off. She shook her head when he asked if Jack had mentioned Hank Crawford or Dusty Wilson. Yet it was enough. Even though his only witness was a dead man, Roman knew where Frank Kessler stood. He led the two burdened horses across the small meadow toward the trail that circled the nearby ridge, and carefully reviewed his plan for the next half-hour.

At the edge of the meadow he slapped the horses downtrail, shouting them on their way. The lead horse, Dobe's own, would not stop until it reached the KK yard. He waved at Laurie and put his gelding directly up the slanting ridge. She followed, and after a climb of fifteen minutes they drew rein on the crest.

Angling down through the pine timber on the ridge's far side, Roman halted after another ten minutes and stepped to earth. He tethered his mount and glanced up at the girl. She nodded before he could speak.

"I know," she said. "I'm to stay here no matter what happens. And if you're not back in half an hour at the most, I'm to ride to Box and tell Ben Fowler everything I know."

She tried to smile, and the pitiful attempt clutched abruptly at Will Roman's throat. He touched her hand. "Laurie," he murmured. "Laurie, please don't—"

"I'm not going to cry," she said. "I'm not going to cry now. I'm going to wait until the whole thing is over and cry for everyone—for all of us, Will."

She bit her lip and turned away. Will slid his carbine from its boot and walked down through the trees. Minutes later he found himself on an outcropping that overlooked the KK yard.

He heard hoofbeats and caught a glimpse of two horses trotting across the meadow toward the outbuildings and corrals. A man stepped down from the porch of the house, moving across the yard. As his yell of alarm rang across the flat Roman slipped down through a small gully. Keeping to the cover of a growth of seedling pine, he raced for the edge of the nearer corral.

He had traversed the length of the pen, unavoidably stirring up the half dozen horses inside, when he heard Frank Kessler's outraged curse and knew the man had discovered the body of his brother. The holding corral, a makeshift affair constructed of unsplit saplings and brush, provided excellent cover. Roman was within fifteen yards of the three men when he stepped into the clear.

Frank Kessler had been staring at the lifeless bodies on the two mounts. He swung about now, dazed. Will stepped farther into the clear. With a swinging motion he sent a silver object flashing in a high arc to land within inches of the rancher's feet. The carbine in his other hand covered Kessler and his two hired men.

"In case you don't recognize it, Frank," Roman called clearly, "that tin star at your feet represents the law on the Judith. It came off the shirt of a deputy named Slim

Olsen, a man whose death you're going to hang for—
unless you want to take your chances now."

The hump-shouldered rancher tilted his head farther
forward, peering at Will from under his brows. It was
a wary, speculative look, and it slid from Roman to the
two gunmen who stood off to one side.

"Boys," Will said, "I'm wearing the authority of that
badge today. You were smart enough to hightail it out
of Miles City when things got too hot, and you're still
alive. I'm giving you that same chance again. The world's
wide, but your friend Bert won't see it from where he's
gone."

"Don't listen to him, boys!" Kessler's voice rose and
cracked. "We've got him three to one! He don't stand a
chance at them odds!"

The two gunnies stood pat, waiting. Roman laughed.

"You boys knew Bert," he said. "Wasn't he supposed
to be a pretty good man with a gun?"

The gunhands looked at the corpses on the two horses.
They exchanged glances. The taller one said, "That hand
looks too rich for my blood," and walked off slowly
toward the three saddled mounts at the rack in front of
the porch. There was a silence, and then his partner followed him. Frank Kessler did not move or speak. He just
watched his two gunnies ride out.

Roman said softly, "Turn around, Frank. Drop your
iron in the dirt. I'll tell you right now, it would make me
damned happy to have to kill you."

Frank Kessler's dark eyes stabbed across the yard at
Will. He made his decision, and then he grinned.

"I reckon it would, at that," he said.

Kessler turned around. He dropped his sixgun to earth.

CHAPTER X

Reno Sinclair rode out of Judith City at sundown. For the past three hours he had been standing at Sid Patterson's bar, watching the diminishing level of the whisky in the bottle before him—the second bottle, because Sid had exchanged a new bottle for the one he'd already emptied.

The new bottle, too, had all but disappeared before he lurched outside, carrying it uncorked in one hand. Later, as he reined up at the river crossing two miles above town, he re-discovered the quart, wondering how he came to be carrying it here on the open range. He laughed, drained it in one long draught and tossed it into the shallows along the brushy bank.

As the big stallion beneath him footed its way across the ford, stubborn sobriety struggled with the alcohol fumes in Reno's brain. Though he had gone over the whole thing time and time again during the past few hours, each renewed perusal of his plan seemed fresh and without repetition.

Ben. There was the crux of the matter. Old Ben. Old bend-down-and-knuckle-under Fowler. Yes sir, old Ben had to go. Why? No matter why. Who cares why? Let's see, how does that go? *Yours not to question why; yours but to.* . . . Well, to hell with that, but. . . . Sure. Sure, there's a why! Always a why, sure! Gonna take over Box and Slash and the whole damned shebang, that's why. Ellen. Good old Ellen. Yes sir, what's yours is mine, ole gal. We'll run this whole damned basin together before we're through. And maybe a hell of a lot sooner

103

than you think. Yes sir, you just leave it to good old
Reno, that's what you do. Yes sir.

Riding up the far, sloping bank of the river, Reno
kicked one leg free of the stirrup, bent it around the horn,
and gave himself over to a sudden, mysterious, but un-
controllable urge to sing. He never knew whether he had
uttered a note, for in the next moment he found himself
flat on his back, staring at the darkling sky. Frowning,
he came up to one elbow. It took him a while to locate
his saddler in the growing dusk.

That last drink . . . ! He cursed and got up. He cursed
some more when the big stallion shied away as he sought
to grasp the reins. Stand still, you damned, worthless
hunk of crow-bait! Finally he got a grip on the reins and
managed to swing into the saddle. He roweled cruelly,
drawing fierce satisfaction from the frightened and pain-
stricken animal's surging reaction to the steel. The stallion covered fully half a mile before Reno relented,
drawing the beast down to a sedate walk. Humor and
exhilaration had fled, and once more Reno attacked the
problem he had built for himself.

The tentative fingers of apprehension did not touch
him until he circled the ranch, coming up behind the
outbuildings and barn on the side nearest the hills. Was
he being a damned fool? No. He wasn't a fool and he
wasn't afraid. He thrust all doubt aside, cursing the
liquor, blaming the liquor for this belated feeling of
weakness.

There was no chance for him here on the Judith as
long as Frank Kessler and Sam Engstrand held him
bound by the heels. And there was but one answer to
blackmail. Power. Total and insurmountable power. The
full power of Box, as well as Ellen's Slash D. The command of the entire Box crew, added to the six men he
had brought north on his own. If Sam Engstrand and the
Kesslers wanted war, then he'd give them war! But
Ben—no doubt about it, Ben Fowler had to go. And it
was a job he could trust to no one but himself. There was
the chance, of course. But, good Lord, man, look at the
stakes!

Reno stepped unsteadily from the saddle and drew his carbine from its boot.

Reno did not even think of Ben Fowler as a human being when he approached the narrow runway between bunkhouse and barn. He had never liked the old man. He would have quit Box long ago if it hadn't been for the chance he saw to marry Ellen Dunbridge. As far as Reno was concerned, Ben Fowler had outlived his time long ago. And yet, strangely, he found himself shaking—shaking so violently that he had to lean against the barn's rough wall.

Until this moment—until the yellow square of Ben's bedroom window came into view directly across the yard—Reno had avoided all thought of Will Roman. But now, seeing the old man sitting upright in bed across the deserted yard, he remembered Will. For some reason a vision of Will fighting his way almost singlehanded to the top of a hill near Chickamauga, appeared full blown upon the screen of his mind. Will, bloody and implacable, the vengeful Rebel, making those Yanks pay. . . .

Reno became conscious of the cotton-dry yet rancid taste of his mouth. He felt by turns burning hot and freezing cold. He raised a shaking hand before his eyes and he cursed silently, bitterly, disclaiming the fear that clutched at his bowels.

If he walked off now, he knew he would have to keep riding. There would never be a turning back for Reno Sinclair if he walked away now.

He chose a spot six or eight feet short of the front of the two buildings. He lifted the carbine and levered a cartridge gently home. Taking an off-hand stance with one shoulder braced against the barn wall, he laid his sights out before him. The whole wide square of the lighted window danced crazily above the rifle's front bead, slowing gradually as a cold sweat broke out on his brow.

Ben's body, Ben's face came into focus. Reno gulped his dry breath and, cheek wed to stock, he contracted his finger and fired.

Terror bounded like a wild thing from its imprisoning cage, overwhelming him. The rifle dropped from his hands as he fled. Sightless, black, the night before him seemed to defy escape. And yet, somehow, he was in the saddle, and somehow distance, that beloved ally of lost and tormented souls, drew its widening margin between him and the madness he had left behind.

Reno Sinclair had made his bid.

He did not know how he reached town, though his caution in avoiding the lights of the street as he swung off into the shadows behind the main buildings was as instinctive as it was unusual for reckless Reno Sinclair. Cold sober now, he could not control the tremors that seemed to shake his whole body. His need for whisky was great.

Stepping down in the darkness behind Patterson's saloon, he left his mount and pushed through the rear door. The back room was dark and he stumbled, cursing the chair that barred his path. He had already gone through the door into the main saloon when he saw his mistake.

Sam Engstrand and all three of his sons stood at this end of the bar, regarding him steadily. Could they see, could they read the guilt in his face? The urge to flee and the desire for drink struggled within him, holding him there before the open door.

Sam Engstrand jerked his thumb at the half empty bottle on the bar.

"Better have one, boy," he said softly. "You look like you're living on borrowed time."

Will Roman and Laurie Carstairs rode into Judith City well after dark. Frank Kessler, hunched silently in the saddle ahead of Will, looked neither to the right nor left as men appeared upon the walks, staring and pointing at the ominous burdens upon the two led horses bringing up the rear. Word of the arrival of the small cavalcade had spread the length of the street before they reached the hotel. Will nodded at Laurie and she swung in to the hotel hitchrack, Roman and Kessler and the trailing mounts continuing on to the sheriff's office and jail.

Lew Brady came to the door and grunted as if someone had poked him in the gut. Roman and Kessler stepped down in unison, Kessler moving at once across the walk and into the jail. Brady lumbered out, heavily timid, to inspect the bodies. Roman started to enter the office.

"Good God," Brady croaked. "It's Dobe Kessler!" While the crowd stared, he ran after Roman and caught his coat. "You sure you know what you're doing, man?"

Will glanced inside, making sure that Frank was standing quietly beside the barred inner door. He nodded briefly at Lew.

"I'm your deputy, Sheriff. You'd better hope I do."

He picked out Amos Flushing, Henry Freeman and two or three ten-cow ranchers in the crowd, realizing that they likely had met here in town to ride out to Box in a body. He said, "Henry, Amos, the rest of you boys —you might stick around over at Ed's a few minutes before you head out to Box. I'll be over and let you know how things stand."

He went inside, hearing the raised jumble of their voices behind his back. Kessler's beady eyes mocked him in the moment before he turned to hobble along the row of cells. Roman pushed back an iron-barred door with the toe of his boot, motioning for Frank to step inside.

"Reckon you'll let 'em know how things stand, eh?" Kessler's grin bared yellow teeth beneath his ragged mustache. "Might be you'd better be doin' a little figuring on that one yourself, sonny boy. When it comes to lawin', you might find you've got a thing or two yet to learn. You'll sweat a long time in hell 'fore you pin anything on me and that's the plain truth."

Roman turned to take the keys from Brady as the sheriff came down the hallway between the cells. He pulled the door to with a clang and shot the bolt home.

"There's a few things I may not be able to prove just yet," he said. "But Jack tied the rope around your neck before he died, Frank." He let his glance run over the cell to the far wall and the barred window which stood at shoulder height above the floor.

"I doubt if anyone thinks enough of you one way or

the other to make the same play you pulled for Jack,"
he continued idly. "But it would be mighty easy for a
man to put a shot through that window—a man, say,
who thinks you might know more than is good for him."

Roman smiled into Frank Kessler's scowl. He said,
"Maybe you killed Hank Crawford and Dusty. Maybe
not. But you know a lot more than you're letting on.
We're leaving that window unguarded, Frank. Lew here
will be up front. Any time that window starts getting on
your nerves, sing out. We'll be glad to hear you talk."

Will followed the sheriff past the other cells to the
office in front. Brady was in a pitiful state.

"I don't know, Will," he said. "I reckon you know
what you're doin'. But me, I figure I'm takin' a mighty
steep chance. I ain't forgettin' what happened to Slim."

Roman tapped the badge on Brady's chest. He said,
"You take your job real serious, don't you, Lew?" And as
he moved to the door, he added, "I'll see if one of the
boys will come over and hold your hand. I wouldn't take
it kindly if you let our bird fly the coop, Sheriff."

Outside, Ab Newton was waiting. A middle-aged man
of mild manners and a habit of coughing before he spoke,
the merchant nodded uncomfortably toward the three
bodies.

"I can have the boy help me knock up the coffins," he
said. "Meantime we'd better lay 'em out in the back of
the store."

"Take care of it, Ab." Will laid his hand on Newton's shoulder. Feeling the merchant's curiosity, he
briefly described the action which had occurred up on
the bench.

"What about you and old Ben?" Ab asked finally.
"Word's got around that you're through at Box. I hear
tell Sam Engstrand's spreading the news you're high-
tailing it out of the country. Some say he's even hinted
he's running you off the Judith himself."

Will was startled. Noting Newton's careful appraisal,
however, he laughed.

"That would be the day, Ab," he said lightly. "It just
might be that Sam will have more serious things to worry

about before this night's through, though you don't need to quote me on that."

He stepped up to the walk in front of Ed Ferguson's saloon. Ruby appeared at the hotel door farther on. At her gesture he turned that way, sensing her impatience. She searched his face carefully.

"I can't get a word out of Laurie," she declared. "You —you didn't kill Jack?"

He shook his head shortly. He started to speak, but hesitated a moment, considering the words he should use.

"She thinks it was her fault," he told her then. "Jack made a damned-fool play. Tried to grab the gun from her hand. He didn't stand a chance. Dobe's hardcase hand let him have it the minute he made his break."

Ruby's lips formed a silent circle of understanding. "Her fault? That's foolish."

"Right. We've got to convince her of that, Ruby."

Glancing sidelong, Roman saw Henry Freeman standing in the open doors of the saloon, looking his way.

"I knew something more than Jack's death was eating at her," Ruby said quickly. "I'll do what I can."

Moving back along the walk, Roman stepped through the batwings behind Henry Freeman. Several townsmen as well as eight or nine ranchers and punchers were standing along the bar. He told them as simply as possible what had taken place at the KK ranch that afternoon. After answering several questions concerning what proof he had of the Kesslers' guilt in both the rustling and recent shootings, he held up a restraining hand.

"Gents," he said clearly, "I know Ben Fowler asked you all to show up for a powwow at Box tonight. And I'm not asking you different. It's after seven now. If you will all stay in town until, say, about nine, I think you'll find that several of the things Ben wants to talk to you about will have smoothed themselves out by then."

After that, Will Roman poured himself a stiff drink.

Laurie obediently finished the steak Ruby had set before her upon the kitchen table. Though tired from the long hours she had spent in the saddle, she knew she would not be able to sleep for some time to come.

Surprisingly, Jack's death had not affected her as lastingly or as deeply as she had feared it might. Somehow, with all that had passed during this last year, Laurie had subconsciously steeled herself against this eventuality. For an hour or so this afternoon she had seemed to float in a haze of shock, of numbness which blocked off any reaction. Since then, however, she had begun to analyze her awakening emotions with a measure of calmness.

As she sat idling over her coffee—Ruby having strenuously objected to her helping with the suppertime rush—Laurie stared blindly across the kitchen, seeking some final answer in the web of the day's events. She had gone upstairs and put little Jimmy to bed as soon as she returned. Now, reliving that drama in which she had seen her husband shot down before her eyes, she went over each small detail as it had occurred.

There was no doubt about it, she realized now: Jack had not intended to use the weapon he tried to take from her hand upon either Dobe Kessler or the hired gunman who had killed him. Jack Carstairs, the man she had married in Texas and the father of her child, had lied even in his dying moments. Actually, instead of being the instrument of her husband's death, she had prevented Jack from killing Will Roman. And the gunman, Bert, would have killed Jack in any case.

In the moment they had struggled before the cabin, Jack's fearful gaze had been turned toward Will. He had been completely oblivious of the man called Bert—the man who, mistaking Jack's motives, had killed him. Dying in her arms, Jack had sworn otherwise, but now Laurie knew he had lied.

And if Jack had lied about one thing, what of the rest? Gasping, he had told her of Reno's part in the rustling, of the Kesslers' plan to hold him as a threat to keep Reno in line. Could she believe this when he had lied about his intentions of helping Will? Reno Sinclair was Will's friend. Could she take the responsibility of planting suspicion in Will's mind against Reno on the

strength of Jack's word? And yet. . . . Laurie glanced
up, surprised to see that Ruby Ferguson had taken the
chair across from her and was studying her closely above
her steaming cup.

"It won't get you any place, you know," the older
woman said. "Blaming yourself never does."

"I'm sorry, Ruby. I—"

"I know. I know. I'm the kind who tromps in where
angels fear to tread, as the saying goes. But I've talked
to Will. He's worried about you. And I don't mind saying I am too."

The woman's obdurate outspokenness touched Laurie.

"I'm not blaming myself," she said. "Perhaps I was for
a while, but—" Suddenly she was blurting it all out, telling Ruby everything she knew or thought. She repeated
what Jack had told her about Reno Sinclair. She asked
Ruby's advice.

Ruby sipped at her coffee, her eyes grown thoughtful.

"I can't say I'm too surprised," she said finally. "Reno
was never one to put much stock in the rights or feelings of others. Still, Jack may have been—" She lowered
her cup to the table with a thump.

"I think you'd better tell him, child. A dying man seldom lies, but maybe Jack didn't know he was dying.
Reno could be in this up to his neck. And unless Will is
told—" She thumped the cup again. "There's no sense
taking a chance."

Will Roman came through the dining room to the
kitchen. He leaned against the doorjamb and smiled
wryly at the two women. "Any chance for a man to
scare up some grub around here?"

Ruby got to her feet and went to the big kitchen range.

"Stray saddlebums and deputies pay in advance," she
told him tartly. "Of course now, if you were working for
some reliable outfit—"

"I guess that lets me out."

He lost his smile as he glanced at Laurie. He came
away from the door, letting himself into a chair on her
right. He felt an unreasoning embarrassment steal over
him. He could not avoid the fact that Jack Carstairs was
dead. He knew he should not be thinking such thoughts,

nor allowing the sweet heaviness of Laurie's mouth, the
full, youthful rise of her breasts beneath her wool shirt,
to dwell in his mind. He was tired, he told himself. But,
thank God, he had not been the man to kill Jack. He
made a deliberate effort to discipline his mind.

"You'll be all right here? You and the boy?" he asked.

"We'll be fine. Don't worry about us, Will. I—"

The sound of footsteps running across the small lobby
and dining room swung her glance toward the door.

Will got to his feet. Ellen Sinclair burst into the room.
She had seen Will from the lobby. She did not pause
now. She threw herself into his arms.

"Oh, Will, Will!" She shuddered against him, her
fingers tightly grasping his arms. "Oh, darling, I'm so
glad you're here! You've got to do something! I—"

Her voice choked off as she clung to him, her body
shaking with sobs. As he held her, Will became conscious
of the outspoken endearment she had used. Over Ellen's
dark head he glanced at Laurie, seeing the high flush
of color that came to her face. When she turned away,
quickly leaving the kitchen, he took Ellen's shoulders
firmly in his hands. Easing her back, he studied the tear-
stained cheeks, the twisted, crying mouth, the frightened
blue eyes. And in spite of the beauty that shone through
her tears and crying expression, in spite of the warm
shapeliness of the body which had pressed so tightly
against him, Will Roman found that he was unmoved.
There was the faintest stir of wonder in him, and then
he let it go.

"Get hold of yourself, lass," he told her quietly. "What's
Reno done now?"

The very lack of sympathy in his words shocked her,
widening her eyes and drawing her mouth more firmly
into shape. She sniffed against tears and shook her dark
head.

"You don't understand. It's Dad—it's Ben, Will. Somebody rode up outside the house and shot Dad!"

CHAPTER XI

The small room at the back of Sid Patterson's saloon, most of which was used as storage for beer and whisky kegs, contained a single round table and several chairs. Reno Sinclair had spent much time at this table during the past two years, involved in various high-stake games wherein the players preferred the privacy of the back room to the more open surroundings of the half-dozen tables in the room up front.

Sitting now beneath the shaded overhead lamp which hung down from the ceiling, Reno was painfully aware of the size of the stakes for which he played. It was, however, no game of his choosing. Or at least, if he had chosen, he had done so unwittingly, some time in the past.

Through the heavy alcoholic fog which befuddled his mind, Reno began to appreciate more than the mere size of the stakes involved. Even as he took another drink from the neck of the bottle before him, he realized vaguely that he was powerless to play his own hand.

There were no cards on the table. The game was not poker, nor were dollars or chips the stakes. The stake, for Reno Sinclair, was the right to rule his own life.

Sam Engstrand smiled across the table at Reno. He was standing, one booted foot planted upon a chair-seat as he leaned forward upon his knee. His older sons, Jere and Matt, flanked him on either side. None of the Engstrands spoke as they watched the storm gather upon Reno's face.

"Well, damn it, speak up! Y'got anything t'say, now's time spit it out!" Reno's words ran together as he glared across the light. Sam's face was in shadow and this angered him more. Though he knew he shouldn't, he took another drink from the bottle he still held in his hand. Engstrand's voice seemed to come from a distance much greater than the few feet between them.

"Sure, boy, I'll speak up. You go right ahead and get yourself a good snoot full. Everything's under control."

Vaguely Reno was aware of the contemptuous grins on the faces of Jere and Matt Engstrand. Beneath the anger and turmoil of his thoughts it came to him that there should have been one more. Young Mark. That was it. What had happened to Mark Engstrand? And, come to think of it, why were these three standing around in a circle watching him like buzzards around a corpse?

The aptness of the simile started sweat at Reno's brow. He writhed inwardly as he remembered Ben Fowler and. . . . The carbine! That was it! He had dropped his carbine somewhere between Box and town! But the effort to shape some solution that would take care of the lost carbine was too great. He took another long pull at the bottle. His thoughts returned to the men before him. A new sense of satisfaction replaced the fear he had felt.

They didn't know Ben was dead. That was his ace in the hole. Let them laugh and jeer. Sure, he was drunk. But he also was the ruler of Box, and that meant the whole damned Judith. Well, he almost was. He would be when things were settled. To hell with the Engstrands. Yes, and to hell with Frank Kessler, too. With the power of Box behind him. . . .

Reno Sinclair was slumped in his chair, grinning foolishly to himself, when the back door opened. Young Mark Engstrand stepped into the room. Glancing at Reno, the boy grimaced with disgust. Then he looked at Sam.

"He's in the third cell back," he said quietly. "The window's high, but there's a couple of boxes in the alley."

Sam Engstrand nodded, returning his foot to the floor. Jere moved toward the door. Sam said, "Not so fast, boy, not so fast," and Jere stopped in midstride.

"What the hell, Pa?" Jere's broad shoulders hunched

beneath his plaid coat. "The quicker we do the job, the better off we'll be. We stand around here much longer and he's liable to shoot off his mouth to Roman or Brady."

"Reckon you don't know Frank," Sam Engstrand said. "Course, we can't take the chance of Roman gettin' him down to Miles City for trial—not after the deal we made with him and Dobe. But there's one little thing you're overlookin'. You think I brought this fancy Dan back here just to pass the time?"

Reno's head had all but fallen forward upon his chest, yet he seemed to sense this reference to himself. He brought his head up, blinking against the light. Sam Engstrand chuckled dryly.

"Hell, boy," he said to Jere, "this whole thing's fallin' right into our plans. Sinclair here's got just as much to lose if Frank talks as we have. Maybe more. It's my idee he'd be just the boy to pull the job."

Reno shook his head. The room whirled dizzily, then straightened. He cast about for the bottle he had been holding, but could not find it. He made an effort to rise, gave it up and collapsed once more into the chair. He strained his eyes against the light, trying to focus on Sam Engstrand's face.

"Pull job?" He drooled the words. "A'ready pulled job. Bigges' job ever pulled. Rammin' Box now, see! Don't take no damned guff f'um nobody, see?"

Sam Engstrand stepped around the table. He slapped Sinclair deliberately across the face, backhanding him a second and a third time with swift, punishing blows.

Reno started up. Sam pressed him easily back into the chair. Blood ran from a break in Reno's lower lip, dripping slowly off his chin.

Sam Engstrand said, "Listen, drunk. Your friend Roman put Dobe Kessler away and tossed his brother Frank in the can. Frank's sittin' over there in a cell right now, just waitin' to spill his guts. That mean anything to you?"

Reno tried to assemble his thoughts. Frank Kessler in jail. But what the hell? Ben was dead. He, Reno Sinclair, was on top. He had nothing to fear . . . or did he? What if Frank talked? What if he told about Reno's part in the rustling last summer? And there was Jack Car-

stairs. . . . Damn! Why hadn't he gone on to get Jack after
that mess with Dusty Wilson? He goggled up at Sam
Engstrand, unaware of the blood that dripped from his
chin.

"What the hell?" he demanded. "It's Frank's word
against mine. I—"

Reno looked into the gleaming bore of a sixgun which
had appeared in Engstrand's hand. The hammer made
a sharp clicking sound beneath Sam's thumb.

"Mister," Engstrand said, "maybe you forget me and
my boys know all about what happened to a friend of
yours. You may be rammin' Box now, but where would
you stand if Roman found out what really happened to
Wilson?"

Reno could not take his eyes from the bore of the gun.
In its bright, hypnotic gleam he saw Dusty before him,
watched Dusty fall from the saddle on the trail. He saw
old Ben's bloated figure, sitting upright in bed atop the
sharp sight of a gun. He felt a stricture at his throat. He
gasped, tearing at his collar. He was surprised when
no binding rope met his hand.

Sam Engstrand stepped back.

"He'll do the job all right," he told Jere. "But maybe
you'd better go along to see he gets it done right."

A grin twisted the still puffed and bruised line of
Sam Engstrand's mouth.

"Yes sir," he said, "I reckon Box and Chair will get
along fine from here on out. Hell, with you in the saddle,
Sinclair, I wouldn't be surprised but what you and me
me could do more business together than you ever
thought of with Frank."

Fear and hatred lay like twin stones in the depths of
Mark Engstrand's soul. Tonight he had feared accom-
panying his father and brothers into town almost as much
as he had feared their reprisal had he refused to
come. There was nothing left in Mark but this fear and
hatred for Sam Engstrand and for Jere and Matt as well.
If it had not been for his mother, who herself lived in
a constant state of anxiety beneath her husband's unpre-

dictable tempers, Mark would long ago have ridden out of the Judith Basin.

This night, however, the resolve was slowly but surely building within him to make the break regardless. Perhaps, if he managed to get away from Sam and his brothers without unduly exciting their suspicions, he would have time to ride out to the ranch and persuade his mother to come with him. If not, he would leave alone.

Before Will Roman had ridden into town with Frank Kessler and the bodies of three other men, he had not had a chance to get away. Urgency and a mounting sense of desperation had arisen within him when he learned for the first time that his father had made some kind of deal with Frank Kessler and therefore could not allow Kessler to remain alive to talk.

The thought of further killing, particularly since he had seen Sam and Jere kill Hank Crawford at the Carstairs place last night, sickened Mark physically. When Reno Sinclair had come into the saloon, Mark had held back, hoping to get away after Sam suggested they all have a talk in the back room.. He had noticed that Sinclair had seemed strangely upset, but had paid little attention to the man. He had just obeyed Sam's nod ordering him along.

Mark knew his father distrusted him as much as he hated his father. Sam considered Mark weak and womanishly opposed to violence, and had kept him under close surveillance since returning home last night. Sam had not openly stated the fact, but Mark knew that his own father would not hesitate to kill him if he thought Mark might turn informer about the Crawford killing. Sam's choice of Mark to ascertain in which cell Frank Kessler was being held, had been both a test and a challenge from father to son.

Now, as Sam, Matt and Mark stepped once more into the long front room of Sid's saloon, Mark glanced nervously at the batwing doors up front. Accepting the beer Sid placed before him in lieu of the whisky his father and brother drank, he caught Sam studying him in the dusty mirror behind the bar. Surprisingly, Sam smiled,

though there was little actual humor in the expression.
One eye wore a blackish green tinge and Sam's mouth
and jaw were still misshapen and discolored from the
beating he had taken at Roman's hands.

"What's the matter, boy?" Sam demanded. "Shiverin'
in your boots? Hell, we got us a better deal with that
weak sister than we ever made up on the bench. Maybe
you better take a look-see out front. Could be some of
them rannies across the street might wander out and
spoil the play."

Mark needed no urging. As he walked toward those
swinging doors he knew what he was going to do. His
horse was standing at the rack beside the others and he
would step up to the saddle and never look back. He did
not realize how fast his heart was beating until his
father's voice reached out and stopped him just as he
touched the batwing door.

"Ain't got no smart ideas, have you, boy?"

A chill ran the length of Mark's spine. Tension
stretched every nerve in his body as he imagined Jere
and Reno Sinclair in the alleyway beside the jail. He
shook his head without turning and pushed on through
the doors.

Will Roman swung out of the hotel's kitchen, leaving
Ellen behind him. The shock which he had felt at the
news that Ben Fowler had been shot was hardly lessened
by the knowledge that the wound had not proved fatal.
During his ride down from the bench this afternoon he
had become convinced that neither Frank nor Dobe
Kessler had taken a direct hand in the deaths of Dusty
and Hank. Of course, this left Sam and his boys, whom
he was sure Dusty had followed up on the bench. Yet
the Engstrands had been here in Judith City since sundown and could not possibly have shot Ben.

And then there was Reno.

Roman could hardly force himself to believe that Reno
would go to such lengths, no matter what he might stand
to gain. Reno might have been mixed up with the Kesslers
in running off a few head of basin stock, but this. . . . No,
he couldn't believe it.

He crossed the small dining room and entered the lobby.

Laurie came down from the stairs, stopping him as he crossed the room. He wondered at her stiff, embarrassed expression. Then he remembered that she had left the kitchen before Ellen had rushed in and announced her news.

"Somebody took a potshot at Ben through the bedroom window," he told her. "Just creased his shoulder, though not from trying."

Laurie's eyes widened. Her self-consciousness slipped away.

She said, "Oh, Will! If only I had told you sooner!"

Then she revealed what Jack had told her about Reno before he died. Will felt a chill creep over his body. Had Reno, too, been up on the bench the night Dusty was killed? Had he lied about riding to Chair and finding Sam and his boys at home? He remembered Sam's smug expression after Reno volunteered that information. He sighed heavily.

"It might be a wise idea to stay off the street," he told Laurie, and went through the bar. Freeman and several small ranchers, were still there. He waved and walked on.

Outside, he glanced down the street. Four Engstrand horses were tied at the rack in front of Patterson's saloon. He stepped into the street's drying mud, and then he saw Mark Engstrand push through the saloon's swinging doors. Looking neither to right nor left, Mark crossed the walk. In three strides he reached his mount and swung up.

Roman stopped, somehow detecting the taut sense of urgency which drove the young rider. Swinging away from the rack, Mark bore toward Roman. In the outthrown light from Newton's store, Roman studied the boy's strained and fearful expression as he came on.

Will stepped directly into the path of the oncoming mount, lifting one hand as he called Mark's name. So startled was Mark that he glanced back at the saloon, failing to see Will there in the half dark street. Yet he did not slacken his pace.

Roman called again to the boy. The horse swerved to

avoid him. He clutched for the bridle, breaking into a half run.

"Damn you, Roman! Let go there!" Mark Engstrand cursed him as Will's grip brought the horse's head down. "Damn it, I'll—"

Roman said, "Easy there, boy," and Mark lashed out with his booted foot.

The blow took Roman full in the ribs. Pain jarred into his chest, but he lunged forward, grasping Mark's coat in his hands. He yanked Mark down from the saddle. Surprisingly, Mark fought him, swinging his arms in wild flailing motions that did little but slide off Will's arms.

Will sidestepped a swinging blow and collared the boy, batting him roughly alongside the head. Instantly all fight went out of Mark Engstrand. He stood docilely in Roman's grasp, tears streaming down his face. Roman relased his hold on Mark's collar and stepped aside to retrieve the boy's mount.

"Things piling up, Mark?" Will spoke gently, knowing the sort of life the kid had endured at the hands of the older Engstrands. More than once he had pitied Mark, wondering why he had not run off long before this.

Mark's voice, when it came, was not gentle. Wiping his face with a coatsleeve, he suddenly gave vent to a steady stream of curses. Will waited until he had run himself down.

Then he said, "What about Hank, Mark? Was it pretty bad?"

Mark stiffened. In the hotel's dim light his pale, strained features seemed to crumple. His shoulders sagged and he hung his head.

"Tell me," Will Roman said.

"Sure, they did it," Mark said. "They did it and I sat there and watched them. Hank, he came out. Said Miz Carstairs wasn't home. He saw us plain, but he wasn't expecting no trouble. Even asked us if we wanted coffee. When he turned away, Jere shot him. Shot him in the back. Dad shot him too, about the same time. And they burned the place."

Mark looked off into the night.

"I couldn't stand no more," he said. "I hit for town and got drunk."

"And Dusty? What about Dusty, Mark?"

For a moment Roman thought the boy had failed to hear him. But Mark had heard him quite well.

"Dusty? Hell, I don't know about Dusty." He turned as though to walk back down the street the way he had come. There was a blankness in his face, an emptiness that was terrible to see. Will reached out to stop him.

"Here's your horse, boy. You were in an awful hurry to get somewhere when I stopped you."

Mark took the reins, but made no move to mount. It seemed as though he had lost all sense of purpose, as though he had forgotten entirely the fear which had coursed through him so short a while before.

Will frowned, genuinely worried about the kid. He started to speak when a single gunshot slapped flatly from some point farther along the street, its echoes racketing loudly against the building-fronts on either hand.

Swung about by the sound, Roman saw the door of Brady's office swing open. The bulky figure of the sheriff ran into the street. Brady saw Will and ran toward him, yelling.

"It's Kessler! Somebody's takin' a shot at him through the window!"

"Get back inside, you fool." Will spun the big man about by the shoulder. "See they don't make another try. I'll handle the alley."

As he ran for the alleyway between the jail and the building next door, Roman saw Sam Engstrand and one of his sons step out on the walk in front of Sid Patterson's saloon. This sight of the rancher, coming so soon upon the heels of the shot, and absolving Engstrand himself from having fired it, brought Will to a sudden halt. In the light from the saloon's front window he could see the cautious but half grinning expression on the man's bruised face. It struck Will that Sam Engstrand was a very dangerous man. His urgent desire to discover who had fired the shot in the alley was blotted out by what he saw in Sam Engstrand's face.

Before he could speak, a second shot roared between the two buildings. Behind Will the crowd had burst from Ed Ferguson's bar, lining the walk on that side. For the space of a fully drawn breath all eyes converged upon the narrow entryway between the jail and the building next door.

It was in this silent moment that a reeling figure stumbled out of the alleyway, coming to a stand upon the walk. Though he held a sixgun in hand it was pointed down at the boards of the walk. His head was down, as if he were staring at his feet.

"Reno!" Ellen Sinclair screamed from the walk before the hotel.

Bystanders restrained the girl from running into the street. Reno Sinclair raised his head. He weaved drunkenly as he stared at Will and Mark Engstrand there in the mud.

"Didn't mean to kill 'im," he said clearly. "Mistake. All a mistake—"

His voice trailed off to a mumble. He took a single step forward and fell headlong, heavily, sprawling, as only a dead man would fall. Will drew a long, gusting breath deep into his lungs, paying no attention as Ellen broke free and ran past him toward the dead man upon the walk. He looked at Sam Engstrand.

"Sam," he said, "I'm placing you and your boys under arrest for the murder of Hank Crawford. I'd advise you not to try for your gun."

Sam Engstrand did not reply to Will Roman. He spoke to his son Mark.

"So you shot your mouth off, eh, boy?" The words held a sense of harsh finality. "Turned on your own flesh and blood?"

Will knew his advice had been useless even before Engstrand yelled his son Jere's name and clawed for the gun on his thigh. Roman came up with his own weapon, throwing himself into the hardening mud as Mark cried out a warning behind him.

Gunfire slammed into the street from the alleyway beside the jail. Ellen screamed anew as Will thumbed off his shot at Engstrand. Will rolled then, not waiting to see the effect of his shot. He looked at the alley.

Beside him, Mark had been hit, but was still on his feet. On the walk beside the jail, Jere Engstrand struggled with Ellen Sinclair. Jere cursed savagely, his second shot going wild as Ellen bit the arm with which he was trying to hold her before him as a shield. Ellen leaped free and Will leveled his gun. He fired twice in rapid succession.

Jere's body spun fully about as the heavy slugs took him, crashing head-on into the rough boards of the jail. Will spun, seeking Sam. Sam had gone down, but he was searching for his fallen gun.

Roman got to his feet. He shouted, "Matt!" and Matt Engstrand stepped hesitantly out through the batwing doors, holding his hands above his shoulders. At Will's direction he kicked Sam's gun into the street, sending his own after it. Roman called for Lew Brady, turning to Mark as the sheriff moved down the walk toward Sam and Matt Engstrand. The boy had been shot through the fleshy part of his arm. He pulled away, stalking off beneath Will's inquiring gaze.

For a long moment Will stood motionless, unaware of the crowd pouring into the street behind him. He saw Ellen got to her feet from where she had fallen upon the walk. He moved toward her. She was staring down at Reno's body, stricken and mute, as he stepped up beside her. She came into his arms then, holding him tightly.

"Oh, Will! Darling, it was all a mistake! Such a horrible mistake!" She pressed against him with the full desperation of her need. "If only you had come south two years ago instead of sending Reno!"

If only. . . . The words, strangely, rekindled but the smallest memory of the need he had known for this same girl throughout these past years. From somewhere beyond, he heard Sam Engstrand's curse and Brady's voice lifted in insistent and obvious authority. He heard a man call Doc Trimble's name, and Doc's briskly impatient answer. His glance strayed across the street to where a slim girlish figure in jeans and a man's woolen shirt stood outlined against the hotel's front window.

Slowly he disentangled himself from Ellen's embrace.
"Yes," he said with no regret whatever. "But I didn't,
Ellen."

He started across the street toward the hotel. Several
men shouted his name. He ignored them. Laurie had
gone back inside, and he hurried his pace in order to
catch her on the stairs.

THE END